Dance of Darkness

To Lola and Cova
Here's to back porch coffee
and tall tales.

DANCE OF DARKNESS

SIGMUND BROUWER

Chariot VICTOR
PUBLISHING
A DIVISION OF COOK COMMUNICATIONS

THE WINDS OF LIGHT SERIES
Wings of an Angel
Barbarians from the Isle
Legend of Burning Water
The Forsaken Crusade
A City of Dreams
Merlin's Destiny
The Jester's Quest

Chariot Books is an imprint of ChariotVictor Publishing,
a division of Cook Communications, Colorado Springs, Colorado 80918
Cook Communications, Paris, Ontario
Kingsway Communications, Eastbourne, England

First Printing, 1997
Printed in the United States of America.
1 2 3 4 5 Printing/Year 01 00 99 98 97

ISBN: 1-56476-274-2

Library of Congress Cataloging-in-Publication Data
Available on request.

AUTHOR'S NOTE

"We as Merlins will now be able to continue our task. Searching and keeping the treasures of knowledge, and passing on that task to future generations. There will be a day when a renaissance, a rebirth of the sharing of ideas, will take all of us forward into the dawning of a better age. Until then, let us ensure that Magnus stands, quiet, unknown, and on guard against the age of darkness."

—*Lord Hawkwood*, A.D. 1314, *Winds of Light, volume VI, Merlin's Destiny*

While *Dance of Darkness* takes place in A.D. 1364, readers of the first seven books of the *Winds of Light* Series will understand it arises from another story which began generations earlier. The events of this book do stand alone as a complete story, but I hope readers will enjoy the chance to see how it more fully fits with the first story told in the other volumes of the series.

In this volume, two generations have passed since Thomas of Magnus defeated the hidden Druids of northern England. During these two generations, Europe has seen drastic and devastating changes.

As a result, the entire feudal system is in upheaval. Soon gunpowder and a new invention, the cannon, will turn warfare into a machine capable of destroying once unconquerable castles. The Holy Roman Church, once unquestioned and supreme, now faces attack from internal corruption and the greed of kings grasping for land and power.

Even Magnus, once protected by its isolation in the moors of northern England, now feels the turbulence of the waves of change.

This turmoil of social, economic, and religious change provides the perfect cover for those who choose to profit from evil. Among them are the Druids, an ancient cult society, which had been driven into secrecy from the time that Caesar conquered Britain, centuries before Merlin and King Arthur established Magnus as a kingdom to stand against darkness.

The *Winds of Light* Series is the story of Thomas, who reconquered Magnus, taking it away from the Druid powers. Now silver-haired, Thomas yearns for peace in his last years with Katherine, his wife. Despite this yearning, Thomas must continue the centuries-old purpose of Magnus.

Thomas must guide new generations of Merlins, sending them into the world in the fight against evil and Druids. Among those Merlins are the sons and daughters of his own sons and daughters, armed with faith in God and the power of the Merlin books of knowledge.

Yet even within the castle kingdom of Magnus, the Druids begin to reclaim some of what they lost in their first battles against Thomas.

For two generations, time has weakened the Merlins. Some have chosen not to fight for truth and good, but for power and greed. Thus, among the Merlin's greatest enemies are those trained with the innermost secrets of the Merlins.

The outcome of the ancient battle against the Druids has never been less certain.

1

NORTHERN ITALY
A.D. 1364

"Dare to wager a Gypsy?"

Bran had heard Marcel issue this challenge dozens of times, in dozens of crowds of peasants, in dozens of market towns. It was like casting bait.

"Spawn of the devil!" an old woman cried out. "Thieves. No good layabouts. Get back on the road."

Bran had heard this before too. He stood among perhaps twenty people. There were housewives, farmers, apprentices, maids, and beggars.

Marcel held a piece of rope above his head. The rest of the rope was wrapped around Marcel's thick body, coiled over one shoulder and under the opposite arm pit.

"One end of this rope there!" Marcel pointed to the tiled roof of an ancient stone building. He moved his arm to point across the cobbled street. "The other end there! And I walk across!"

Marcel paused. His black eyes glittered in the midafternoon sun.

Bran wished he could wear the same arrogant manner. Bran

wished he had the same dark good looks, the same heavily mus-
cled body. At twenty-one, Marcel was a man in his prime.

Bran? He was sixteen years old. No amount of wishing could
give him the power and command that Marcel held among the
Gypsies.

Bran was small. Fair-haired. He rarely spoke above a whisper.
That alone made him an outcast among the Gypsy families.

There, too, was the matter of Bran's entrance into the Gypsy
world. His mother, a Gypsy princess had died from the Black
Death, barely a day after giving birth to Bran. This ill omen had
cast a dark shadow on Bran. Another baby might have received
sympathy for entering such a harsh world without a mother.

Not Bran.

For his father had not been a Gypsy. Those from outside the clan
were hated and distrusted; Bran's father had done far worse than
most strangers. He had taken the Gypsy princess away to be married in the church. Nearly a year later she had returned without
the outsider, swollen with Bran, ready to give birth, and in the
final stages of the dreaded plague.

It was all Bran knew about his parents. Neither remained to care
for him. Both had left Bran an inheritance of disgrace, something
for which Bran daily paid among his gypsy brethren.

"I shall walk across this rope!" Marcel repeated. He stood upon
the back of a wagon, and none nearby could fail to notice him or
his family members sitting on the wagon behind him. "And I shall
be blindfolded."

More peasants, farmers, and idle townspeople gathered. It was
a hot day. Bran smelled bodies which had not been washed for
months, waste thrown onto the cobblestone from houses, and
manure from cattle driven down the streets.

Bran took refuge in his mind by thinking of cool nights and fires
banked outside the Gypsy tents. He thought of his quiet world in
the shadows outside the Gypsies who sat in circles around the

fires, and how those moments seemed to bring him what little sanctuary he could ever find in a day.

"Yes, blindfolded!" Marcel said, "I will juggle three eggs as I walk from one side to the other!"

"What is your wager?" someone finally called from the crowd.

Despite his lonely thoughts in the midst of a growing crowd, Bran smiled. Always, there was one voice to ask that simple question. And so the hook was set.

"Why, if I drop one," Marcel said, "every person gathered to watch will collect ten lire."

The noise of the crowd swelled into excited babble.

"Quiet! Quiet!" a man shouted. Bran, on his tiptoes to see above the shoulders of the people around him, caught a glimpse of this new speaker.

He was wide and red-faced beneath a dark beard, wearing the luxurious colors of a wealthy shopkeeper. A circle of hair ringed his bald head.

The crowd obeyed his command. This man, Bran decided, was one of the town's respected leaders. Perhaps a mayor.

"If you drop an egg," the man said, "you will pay ten lire to every person gathered."

"That is so," Marcel said.

"Blindfolded, walking across a rope, juggling three eggs."

Marcel smiled. "If you like, have men beneath with pitchforks pointed upward at me. So if I fall, I impale myself."

Crowd noise began to rise.

The shopkeeper raised his hands to keep the noise down.

"You announced this as a wager," the shopkeeper said. "Not a contest. What, then, is the wager?"

Marcel waited until every eye in the crowd was upon him. It grew so quiet that the only sounds were of squawking chickens in the market stalls further down.

"What, then, is the wager?" Marcel said. "The only fair wager possible."

Again, he paused.

Bran admired Marcel's showmanship. Marcel knew how to play a crowd.

"If I succeed," Marcel said. "Each of you gathered pays me ten lire."

People in the crowd turned to each other to trade their views on this.

Marcel did not ask for silence. Instead, he held up a small leather pouch, bulging with coins. Heads turned back to him. Mouths shut.

"Is ten lire not a fair price to pay for entertainment? After all, I risk not only my hard-earned coins, but my very life!"

Bran knew with certainty that the wager would occur.

Few were the opportunities for entertainment. These were not men and women of royalty, able to hire musicians, throw extravagant feasts, or travel with bodyguards to summer estates near the sea. Instead, these simpler poor folk lived their entire lives within the town walls, or on farms within a half-day's walk from the town. A hanging was entertainment for them, as were drunken brawls. Or the spectacle of chasing Gypsies.

They would take the wager, simply for the chance to watch someone risk falling onto pitchforks.

Bran knew, too, what was going through the minds of most of these townspeople.

Gypsies, they would think with scorn. *If he drops an egg, we will make him pay. If he succeeds, we will not pay, but run him and his clan out of this town. After all, they are only Gypsies.*

"I will take that wager," said the wealthy shopkeeper with a greedy smirk. "Any others?"

All in the crowd raised their hands and voices.

"So be it!" the shopkeeper shouted to be heard above them. "Prepare the rope."

2

In the half hour it took Marcel to secure the rope from roof to roof, the crowd beneath tripled, buzzing with speculation.

On the wagon nearby, the Gypsy families watched in silence. Other members of the clan sold simple wooden toys from a makeshift stall in the market. And the remaining Gypsies were back in camp, in a field some half mile from the town.

Bran was the only Gypsy not in the company of others. He was accustomed to this solitude. He was also accustomed to wearing drab rags, while all the other gypsies wore gaily patterned shirts and silky pantaloons. Among them, he was like a little brown sparrow hopping out of the way of larger, prettier birds.

And among the crowd gathered in the market square, Bran was just another poor peasant, of little worth and far beneath anyone's notice.

Which is why the Gypsy clan kept Bran in drab rags. With his dirty blond hair and paler skin, no one would possibly believe Bran was a Gypsy. Nor would anyone treat him with the suspicion accorded to all Gypsies. This sparrow-like appearance made

Bran very valuable to his clan.

Finally, Marcel was ready. He stood on the edge of one roof and bowed to the entire crowd.

The wealthy shopkeeper had arranged for large men to stand beneath the rope, armed with pitchforks. Perhaps he did not mean to see Marcel hurt but only wanted men ready to exact payment when Marcel failed. Or perhaps he truly wanted Marcel impaled at the slightest misstep. It was hard to say. Such was the life of a Gypsy.

"There are now many more of us!" the shopkeeper shouted upward. "You will still pay each of us ten lire?"

"Most certainly," Marcel said, teeth gleaming in a wolf-like grin. "As you will all pay me if I succeed?"

"Yes, yes," the shopkeeper said impatiently. "Begin."

With a flourish, Marcel pulled out a thin, dark strip of cloth. He tied it over his eyes and behind his head. Bran doubted any in the crowd could see what Bran knew. Marcel had positioned the blindfold over his nose in such a way that he could easily peer downward.

Marcel held out three eggs in one hand.

He took his first step onto the rope. It sagged slightly, but held his weight.

"Juggle!" someone shouted. "Juggle!"

Marcel tossed the first egg in the air. Then the second. Then the third. Without walking ahead, he juggled them in perfect rotation until he was comfortable with the rhythm.

Bran had seen Marcel keep six eggs in the air. This was nothing for him.

The crowd, of course, did not know this. They watched in total concentration as Marcel finally took another step on the rope. And another.

Before Marcel was a quarter of the way across, the crowd began to shout and jeer. They did not want to see him complete the balancing act.

The men below began to jab their pitchforks upward. And the jeering grew louder.

Bran had no doubt Marcel would succeed. But Bran did not pause to admire his clansman's great athletic ability.

No, the jeering of the crowd meant Bran, too, must begin his task.

He moved beside a farmer whom he had spotted earlier. This farmer had a small leather bag hanging at his waist from a strap at his shoulders. Bran slipped his hand into the bag and withdrew half the coins inside. To remove all the coins might lighten the bag too much.

As Bran moved on, he tucked the coins inside a leather bag inside his own shirt.

He eased himself through the pressing crowd, stepping close to a housewife he had marked. She, too, had a purse easily plucked.

Bran kept moving through the crowd, picking the pockets of victim after victim. It was simple. All attention was on Marcel. People jostled each other in close quarters. Bran had deft, quick hands, capable of stealing under far trickier conditions. Here, with the noise and the bumping, it was impossible to detect his actions.

In the center of the rope, Marcel paused. He pretended to sway dangerously. He almost dropped an egg.

It was intentional, of course. All of this had been set up to allow Bran to fleece these simple people. Marcel simply wanted to give Bran as much time and opportunity as possible to continue taking coins from unguarded purses.

Marcel resumed his balancing act, getting closer and closer to the other roof, juggling as he walked.

Bran slipped out of the crowd, toward a crooked side street. This was the time he must escape.

Marcel hopped onto the far roof, pocketed the eggs and untied the blindfold. Already, the crowd was beginning to leave, Bran streaming away with a half dozen men and boys.

"What is this?" Marcel shouted with pretended outrage. "You wagered and lost fairly! Return! Return!"

"Gypsy fool!" the wealthy shopkeeper replied. "How do you propose to force payment?"

The men with pitchforks ringed the shopkeeper and looked purposefully upward at Marcel. It was a show of force which made anything Marcel might answer seem totally hollow.

"This is not fair!" Marcel cried. "I might have been killed. Had I dropped an egg, I most surely would have been forced to pay my end of the wager."

"Shut your mouth and be grateful we let you live," the shopkeeper said. "As it is, you have outworn your welcome. You and your families move on, before we take action upon you."

Bran did not hear the end of the conversation. Nor did he need to. It always played out this way. They were only Gypsies, after all. No citizenship. No homes. No protecting soldiers. Spat upon. Feared as messengers of black magic. And used by parents to frighten children. "Behave," mothers would cluck, "or Gypsies will steal you in the night to take you to faraway lands."

Bran walked slowly, careful to press his arms into the heavy, newly-filled pouch resting against his stomach. It would do no good to allow a jangle of coins. It would do no good to drop the pouch and spill coins across the road. For if it happened and some peasants reached for their own pouches to make certain their own coins were safe . . .

Pickpockets were sometimes hung without trial. Bran knew that.

Each time he and Marcel played this game, Bran fought the sour fear in his stomach. All it would take was a single mistake and—

A hand grabbed Bran's shoulder.

"Come with me," came the low voice.

Bran spun around to see a man wearing a hooded cloak. Shadows cast his entire face into darkness.

"Let go of my shoulder," Bran said. The sourness in his stomach grew heavier. "I have no business with you."

"I think you do," the hooded figure said. "Or shall I raise a public outcry and be declared a hero for catching the lad who boldly thieved among the crowd?"

3

Bran hesitated.

This was a large man with powerful shoulders, the sloping muscles obvious despite the heavy clothing. The man's fingers on Bran's shoulder seemed capable of squeezing a rock into crumbled dust.

Yet strength meant nothing if the pursuer no longer held the prey. Bran decided he could outrun this man. And if not outrun, at least dodge him. More than once, Bran had darted away from pursuers, his life depending on his fleetness and agility.

Yet if the man cried for help and the entire town gave chase, could Bran escape? The streets ahead were narrow and crooked, a double-edged sword. As easily as these streets gave him opportunity to spin and twist away, they could also run him into an alley which ended dead. This town, as with all towns, was strange to Bran.

The hand upon his shoulder dropped away.

"Run if you think it will serve you," the hooded man whispered. "For I can see the thoughts upon your face. But I will find you later as effortlessly as I found you now."

Stragglers passed them by, uncaring of the conversation of strangers.

"What is it you seek?" Bran asked.

The man in the cloak laughed. "I could just as well ask it of yourself. What is it you seek?"

Bran clutched his arms tighter to himself, feeling the edges of the stolen coins against his belly. He wanted to spin this conversation into a dance which might give him time to allow his wits to find a way to escape. "What would any man seek but wealth and ease of living?"

The hooded man laughed again. "You answer my question with a question. Any man might seek wealth and ease of living, but you have not declared that as your own dream. Are you any man? Is wealth and ease of living what you seek?"

"And you," Bran said, "also answered my question with a question. What is it you seek?"

"Well spoken," the man said. "I can see your father in you. I want to help you. Now answer my question. What do you seek. Of what do you dream?"

My father in me? Bran felt as if his heart had been prodded with a hot iron. *This man knew my father?*

"My dreams," Bran said, keeping his face still despite the swirling questions inside him, "are my own matters. Not to be shared with a stranger who does not even show his own face."

"I will answer, then, at the proper time," the man said. "Perhaps tonight, when we meet at the bridge along the stream, when the town bells ring midnight."

"How do I know this is not some sort of trap?" Raised around Gypsies, Bran had been taught to keep eternal suspicion.

"If it is harm I want to bring upon you," the man said, "all I need do is call and you will be taken away for stealing from the pockets of the townspeople."

The man shrugged, which moved the hood slightly.

Bran saw, or imagined he saw, a reddish blond beard.

"Besides," the stranger said, dropping his shrug. "What could you, a poor Gypsy boy, have of value for me to steal? Tonight, you shall see that it is an offer of help that I bring."

"Why are you so certain I will appear?" Bran asked, although already he knew he would go as asked. *If this man knew his father. . . .*

"Your curiosity will drive you to it. You wonder how it is I knew you picked the pockets of these townspeople. You wonder why I do not call for your arrest. You wonder about your father. And you wonder what it is that I will offer as help."

"Perhaps," Bran said.

"As you say," the hooded man's voice was low. And amused. "Until then, ponder my question. What is it you seek?"

4

Gypsies were never welcome near towns. To return, then, Bran had walked a mile into the countryside with the heat of the sun on his back. As he arrived at the Gypsy camp, he noted with surprise that he did not remember a single step of his journey through the fields and over stone fences.

The stranger had known Bran's father!

Bran barely noticed the familiar setting in front of him. Although the countryside changed week by week, the Gypsies always set their tents up in the same manner. An inner circle and an outer circle. Room for the wagons that carried their belongings from town to town. Wooden posts driven into the ground to tie goats. Mules hobbled and grazing in the grass beyond. Iron pots hanging over the gray scars of dead ashes created by the nightly fires.

The stranger had known Bran's father!

Unconsciously, Bran let his fingers play lightly with a small medallion hanging from a leather strap around his neck. His father had given it to his Gypsy princess mother in his dying moments. She in turn, had left it for Bran. It was the only possession that linked Bran to his long-dead parents.

The stranger had known Bran's father!

How many nights had Bran fallen asleep wondering the simplest things about his father! From what land had he come to travel here? What had been his destination? What kind of man had he been?

Not one of the elder Gypsies ever spoke of Bran's father or mother, and Bran had learned very young not to ask, for his questions were answered at best with dark looks, at worst with blows to the head.

Bran had decided his father must have been handsome and dashing, perhaps even rich. For how else could an outsider have stolen the heart of a Gypsy woman?

Bran had decided their love must have been of the power and strength to match any ballad. Why else had his mother chosen him over her own people and their strong, clannish ties? Why else had his father risked his life to court her, and risked it even more to take her away? For Bran had heard of how fiercely the Gypsy men protected their women from the outsiders, to the point even of execution. How much more they would have fought to keep a Gypsy princess among the clan.

The stranger had known his father!

Bran was so deep in thought and hope that he failed to hear footsteps behind him. His first warning of trouble was the stinging whack of a branch rod against his back.

"Lazy idler!" came the screech.

Bran spun around.

Bran's first reaction was anger at his stupidity for allowing this to happen.

His attacker was the old great-grandmother of the clan, tiny in a long, black dress, her toothless face little more than a lump of puckered flesh. During the day, she wandered camp, muttering curses at imagined enemies. At night, she squatted in a hunch over a tiny fire, rocking back and forth on her heels as she sang tuneless songs.

"Bring her back," the old woman wailed. She swung the stripped branch at Bran. He jumped out of her reach easily. "Her life belongs with us."

The addled old woman believed it was Bran himself, not his father, who had taken away her Gypsy princess granddaughter. As often as she could, she would pounce on Bran and attack with these same demands.

Bran never lost his temper at the old woman's meanness, but only felt sympathy for her and her poor, addled mind. What pain she must bear, believing Bran's mother still alive, and always searching for the young woman who would never return to camp.

As she took another swing at him with the switch, Bran jumped away. He dug into the pouch of coins beneath his shirt.

He offered her the coin, choosing not to speak.

"Bribery!" she screeched. "You cannot buy her from us!"

She took the coin anyway, holding it in the sunlight to examine the silver. With her attention off him, Bran took slow careful steps as he backed away from her.

Rarely did Bran actually run from one of her attacks, although he could easily have left her and her tottering steps far behind. The few times he had escaped her that way, her wailing and screeching rose as if he were striking her. And with her bad eyesight, there was a good chance she might fall and break her fragile bones as she chased him. Better, then, to stay and take her abuse so that she did not hurt herself.

Bran eased back farther as she examined the coin. The best way to leave her was to distract her, then steal away to. . .

A large hand grabbed the back of Bran's neck.

"So, you worthless dog, you might give away my coin?"

5

Again, Bran's first reaction was anger at himself. This time he would suffer more punishment than a whack from a stick wielded by an old woman. For Bran didn't have to turn around to know who held him.

It was Marcel's father—Antonio—a large man with red eyes and broken veins on his nose. Marcel's father spent most of his nights drinking sour wine. During the day, he had a constant headache, and his temper reflected it.

Antonio cuffed Bran with his free hand. "Give me the pouch."

As Bran reached for the coins, he didn't allow himself to whimper. He never did. Not around Marcel. Not around Antonio. Not around any of the Gypsies. He had long stopped crying, even during the lonely nights.

Antonio took the pouch with a surly grunt. He held the pouch between his teeth, and with both hands shook Bran, listening for the jingle of any coins hidden in Bran's clothes.

Still with the pouch in his mouth, he patted Bran to make the search complete. Antonio's hand stopped at the medallion around

Bran's neck, then moved on. Everyone in the camp knew about Bran's keepsake—Antonio did not mistake it for a coin Bran might have tried to keep. And the medallion was the one thing no one ever tried to take from him. Gypsies were too superstitious to risk violating something as important as a token left behind by the dead.

When he was satisfied that Bran had not kept any coins, Antonio dropped the pouch from his teeth and caught it in his right hand. With his other hand, he cuffed Bran again, and gave him a kick to send him on his way.

"Mongrel!" Antonio said. "Any other Gypsy would have plucked double from those stupid geese of townspeople."

Bran knew Antonio was lying. No Gypsy had quicker lighter hands than Bran, and many secretly envied him for his talent.

"You don't even earn what we feed you," Antonio continued. "You're lucky we don't leave you behind."

Bran walked away with as much dignity as he could. He didn't look back to see if Antonio was following to cuff him again, which happened more often than not.

"Get to the stream," Antonio snarled. "The women need help washing clothes. If I see you idling around camp, you'll get more of the back of my hand."

Bran obediently turned toward the stream.

When he was safely away from Antonio's sight, Bran allowed himself a smile. Beneath his tongue, was a coin that Antonio had been unable to find. Bran would add it to the many he had collected, one by one, over the last years.

Knowing he had fooled Antonio was the only consolation Bran could take, however. The blows still stung and reminded him how much worse it could get if he disobeyed Antonio.

He did not expect to fare better at the stream. As always, the women would mock him for his fair skin and the dishonor of being fathered by one who wasn't a Gypsy.

And tonight, he would get the few scraps left after all the Gypsies had eaten their fill. He would be forced to eat alone in the shadows beyond the fire.

As he walked toward the stream, Bran remembered the stranger's question.

What did Bran seek?

A home.

6

This night, as usual, Bran outwaited the talk at the fires in the shadows beyond. He strained his ears to hear beyond the talk, counting the strikes of the bell that echoed from the town. When the bell struck eleven times, he began to feel restless. He was tempted to bolt camp then, except there were occasions when the Gypsy elders called him to answer drunken accusations of laziness by Antonio. Tonight, Bran did not want his absence noticed. So he forced himself to wait.

The crackling wood finally became dull embers, and the last of the Gypsies shuffled into their tents. Finally, Bran slipped away from the camp.

He trotted slowly through the fields, letting his eyes adjust to the dim light from the moon and stars.

Night held no fear for Bran. He almost thought of it as a friend, especially during the warmth of summer when he often roamed alone beneath the stars, taking pleasure from the soft air and the smell of fields and buzzing of insects. At night, Bran thought of himself as a cat, padding lightly, alert to any sounds, and part of the rhythm of the breeze and swaying grass.

Because he had been forced to waited until all the Gypsies had left the campfires, Bran was late when he reached the road at the river. He wished he could have arrived earlier, to wait in the shadows to see if the hooded stranger arrived alone. Bran was not prepared to believe that anyone in the entire world might wish to help him, and there were too many questions to be answered before he might trust the stranger.

The last peals of the midnight bells had faded from the night air long before he finally reached the bridge. When Bran stepped out from the trees near the road, he saw no one.

He stepped farther into the road, leaving the safety of those comforting shadows.

Still, he saw no one.

A groan reached Bran.

It came from the bridge!

The stones of the bridge formed an arch that rose from the road. The arch fell again on the other half of the bridge. The groan came from beyond, on the side of the bridge hidden to Bran.

He did not want to commit himself to stepping onto the bridge. Although Bran did not fear the night, he knew well the dangers of others who used the night. From his life among the gypsies, Bran knew well that highwaymen preyed on lone travelers. Bridges were one of the best places for highwaymen to ambush the unwary as they hurried to the town so near.

The groan grew louder, then faded into a sigh.

Was this a trap?

Bran thought of the man's words earlier in the day. *If it is harm I want to bring upon you, all I need do is call, and you will be taken away for stealing from the pockets of the townspeople. What could you, a poor Gypsy boy, have of value to steal? Tonight, you shall see that it is an offer of help that I bring.*

If the stranger had wanted to harm Bran, he would have done so earlier.

Bran also thought of the reddish-blond beard that he thought he had seen beneath the man's hood. A traveler from a land far away? His father's land.

Bran would help, then.

As another groan began from the darkness on the other side of the bridge, Bran moved forward.

A few steps later, he saw the fallen figure of a man, half hidden against the wall of the bridge.

The stranger?

Bran hurried close and knelt beside the man.

"Is it you?" Bran asked. "The one with a promise of help?"

The man attempted to roll toward Bran. His head fell back.

Bran lifted the man's head from the cold hard stones. Bran felt slick warmth against his fingers.

Blood!

"Yes, it is I," the man whispered. "Betrayed. The evil ones somehow knew I found you."

"Evil ones?" Bran echoed. "Who is it you fight?"

"We fight them," the man groaned. "It is your fight too."

"My fight? But—"

"No," the man said with sudden strength. "You must run! Now! For if they return. . ."

He clutched at Bran's arm. "The girl will find you. Listen for one word. Merlin."

"Merlin?"

"When you hear it, trust her."

Bran froze. Above the hoarse whispers of the fallen man, his ears had caught the shuffling of leather against stone.

"They have returned," the man said. "I told them you had come and gone, but they have returned. Now run!"

Bran hesitated.

"Run," the man said, "It is not you they want, but your medallion."

The man pushed Bran away.

But it was too late.

From one side of the bridge, two men appeared in outline against the night sky. And then two from the other side.

7

What frightened Bran most was the silence of the men on each end of the bridge. They advanced slowly, as if with total certainty of purpose, total certainty that their prey was in their grasp.

In this silence and fear, everything seemed magnified to Bran. The gurgle of the small river beneath the bridge, the wheezing for breath of the fallen man, the pounding of Bran's heart. All reached him clearly as time ceased to pass.

Step by step the men grew closer.

Bran measured his distances. With two men abreast, the bridge was too narrow to allow room to dodge between them. The drop to the river was too far, and the water too shallow.

At five steps away on each side, the men stopped.

Bran backed himself to the wall of the bridge, trying to keep them in his vision to his right and left.

All four men withdrew short swords from their capes.

"The medallion, Gypsy boy," said one of the men in a soft, deadly voice. "We mean to have it."

Bran could not imagine what importance the small medallion

might have. Yet here were five men—four attacking, one fallen and motionless—who had suddenly appeared in Bran's life as strangers. All of them sought the medallion. To them, it must have great value.

Yet Bran was not going to give it up. To him, it had more value. It was the only thing his parents had left him.

With a sudden flash of insight, Bran knew, too, it was now the one thing which could lead him to the secrets of his parents' lives. For whatever the secret of the medallion, it was a secret they had kept before dying. And if these men knew of the medallion, they must also know of his mother and father.

"I do not have it with me," Bran said. "It is back among the Gypsies. Tell me why you seek it, and I shall bring it to you tomorrow."

One man laughed. "Gypsies never tell the truth, even half-Gypsies fathered by a runaway knight. If we let you go, we'll never see you again."

Fathered by a runaway knight. What else could Bran discover?

Bran ignored the glint of moonlight on their short swords. "My father did not run away," Bran said, thinking as quickly as he could. "He was sent on a mission of great importance."

"Bah," another said. "It was doomed from the beginning. Once he reached Rome, there was one who would have stopped him."

"Enough!" barked the first man. He directed his next words at Bran. "The medallion. We know you carry it around your neck."

Despite the danger which sent prickly sweat down his spine, Bran felt a surge of triumph. He had outwitted them into telling more about his father. A knight who truly *had* been on a mission of great importance.

Bran's mind whirled. Could he fool these men again?

Slowly, he moved his left hand into his shirt pocket, hoping the darkness would conceal the motion of his fingers.

"Do not delay," the first man said. "Whether we take it from you dead or alive, we will take it."

"How is it you know I carry it?" Bran asked, easing his hand away again.

"We know. It is around your neck, on a strip of leather lace. Give it now."

With a sudden spin, Bran hopped onto the bridge wall. The drop to the black water below dizzied him.

"Jump, then," the first man sneered, taking a step forward. "We'll strip the medallion below from your broken body."

Bran did not jump. He reached into his shirt and pulled the medallion over his head. He dangled it in front of them.

"And if I throw this far into the river?" Bran asked. "You will never find it."

The man stopped. "Do that, and you will only live long enough to follow it into the water."

"I wish to live," Bran said. He held the medallion over the water. "Yet before I give it to you, tell me about my father."

"No!" the man on the ground groaned. "At the cost of your life, keep the medallion from them."

Bran tried to ignore the fallen man.

"Tell me about my father," Bran said. "A knight from where?"

"England," came the answer. "The wild moors north of York."

"What was his mission?"

"No more," the first man answered. "I tire of your games. Hand us the medallion and we will let you live. After all, our fight is not with you."

But it is, Bran vowed silently, for any fight of my father's is now a fight of mine.

"You may have it," Bran said. With one hand on the medallion, and the other on the leather strap, he yanked and snapped it loose.

The man stepped closer and held out his hand.

"No. . ." the fallen man groaned.

"Here it is," Bran said.

He tossed it far over their heads. A few seconds later, a rolling clink was heard as it landed on the cobbles of the road.

Two of the men turned at the sound.

It was all the distraction Bran needed.

He dove from the wall toward them and landed in a rolling somersault. Pain shredded his shoulder, but he kept moving. In a flash, he reached his feet and dodged past the men.

Something seemed to touch his arm, burning a long slice through his skin.

A sword!

Bran sprinted.

Something plucked at his shirt, then landed with a clank ahead of him.

A thrown dagger!

Bran twisted and sidestepped, not losing speed. He ran a broken pattern to the end of the bridge, dreading a blade into the back of his ribs at any moment.

None came.

Bran burst from the bridge and ducked hard into the trees along the road. He plunged through brush, climbed over a stone wall, and ran into the field. He felt like his feet were guided by angels, and he skimmed over the soft, grassy earth.

Finally, when his throat and lungs were raw, he allowed himself to look back.

No pursuers.

He had lost them.

Except they knew too much about him. They'd known about the medallion. They'd known where he kept it.

That information could only come from one place. The Gypsy camp. Someone in the clan had betrayed him to a hated outsider.

It meant whatever miserable home that Bran had once had among them was no longer safe.

8

Curled against stacked hay in a field beyond the Gypsy camp, Bran slept poorly . The side of his forearm hurt badly from the thin wound caused by the sword. Whenever he rolled in his sleep, the movement cracked the new crust of dried blood and woke him. Each time he opened his eyes, the fright of his near death took him back to his night at the bridge and all the questions arising from it.

The hurt stranger. Was he truly a friend? If he was, how could it be that they shared the same fight? And what was the fight?

The four men on the bridge. Why did they want the medallion so badly? Who were they? How did they know of his father?

Behind all those questions, Bran did find some satisfaction. He now did know more. His father, a knight! On a mission from England! Comforted by this, Bran felt much less an orphan.

Finally, when pain woke him to the gray beginnings of a new day, Bran sat and hugged his knees toward him. Distant roosters crowed triumph at first discovering the miracle of a rising sun. The gray sky brightened to blue, and still Bran did not move.

He was tired, hungry, thirsty, and his stiff muscles ached with the night cold that had not yet left his bones. But he would not move unless a peasant farmer happened to stray toward this particular stack of hay.

Bran would wait until the Gypsies packed their tents and cleared camp. That it would happen on this day, he was certain. Always, the Gypsy clan departed the morning after Marcel's act upon the rope. The townspeople would have rightfully blamed the Gypsies for their lightened pockets. With only suspicions instead of proof, however, it would take the entire day for them to build their anger and courage to the point of approaching the camp in the evening, usually armed with pitchforks and clubs. They would, of course, find nothing but ashes of fires, bones of chickens stolen from their farms, and grass matted where the tents had stood.

Bran, too, intended to arrive at a deserted camp. But he intended to arrive long before the townspeople. And he expected to find more than ashes and bones. He would reclaim what belonged to him.

9

"Do you need help?"

Although Bran felt his heart leap inside him like a startled rabbit, he forced himself to straighten slowly to the soft, pleasant voice behind him.

A young woman's voice.

He put calm on his face before turning. After all, if she had meant immediate harm, she would have acted instead of spoken. Whatever Bran answered to her, he preferred to do so without showing weakness of fear.

Bran finally faced her. Behind him was a fire pit, long cold since the departure of the Gypsies. In his hand, he held the broken stick he had been using to dig in the ashes.

"There is blood upon your clothing," she said, "and straw in your hair. You stir a fire, yet I see no flames. I find all of this curious."

His questioner was of that graceful age between woman and girl. She wore the fine clothes of royalty and sat astride a white horse. Her hair was long and reddish blonde, tied neatly behind her shoulders.

Bran almost bowed to her, such was her manner.

"I am sorry to be an intruder on your field," Bran said, assuming she was the daughter or wife of the landowner. "I shall leave immediately."

"Before or after you find what you sought in the dead fire?"

Bran kept his face frozen. He did not want his expression to betray how badly he needed what was hidden in the earth below the ashes.

"Do not answer," she said with the trace of a smile at his discomfort. "Instead, let me ask again. Do you need help?"

"I need nothing from any person," he said. "Except solitude."

"I find that an interesting lie. How do you intend to flee the four men who approach on horseback?"

She pointed behind him. He followed her arm with his eyes. He saw only the stone fence at the distant edge of the field and the rising hills beyond.

"There are no horsemen," he said.

"Were there not four men last night?"

How did she know?

"And if I could find you so easily," she said, "so, too, shall they. Where else would you go but to this camp? They will be on horses and coming from the town."

"Who are you?" Bran said, suddenly afraid.

"Your guardian angel."

Bran shrank from her.

She laughed. "It is only a figure of speech. I am sorry. I had forgotten how strongly the Gypsies cling to superstition."

"You are here to guard me?" he asked.

"In a manner of speaking, yes." She smiled. "Those men on horseback, as you will find out soon, seek the medallion."

Medallion. Bran immediately became guarded. If she knew about the medallion. . .

He looked beyond her to the trees along the stream at the other side of the field, and the faraway woods past the stream.

"Were I you," she said, reading his mind, "I would not flee. Yes, before they arrive, escape is likely. Yet escape will not ease your problem. No matter where you travel, their spies will find you. Like hounds on a fox, those four would seek you day and night until they run you to earth in whatever den you chose. They will not rest until they have the medallion."

"I cannot give them what I do not have," Bran said. "Last night, I tossed it into the darkness."

"You tossed a coin. It showed shrewdness on your part. And I admire you for it."

How did she know this? And so quickly?

"I cannot give them what I do not have," Bran repeated. First a hooded stranger. Now this woman on horseback. Both with questions about the medallion. The mystery overwhelmed him. His best path seemed to be in clinging to his own secrets.

"They, however, believe you still have it," she said, "They will torture you until you give it up to them. Or until they are satisfied you do not have it."

"What do you know of the medallion?" Bran asked. "Why do you offer help?"

"The story is far too long to tell now," she said. "If you want to hear it, you must travel with me."

"Where?"

"That, too, is part of the story I shall tell as we travel."

"No," Bran said. His muscles ached. He was cold, hungry, and thirsty. He was tired of these games with words. He trusted her as little as he did the four men the previous night. Perhaps she was trying to get with honey what they had failed to take with swords and threats. "I will find my own way."

"To where?" she asked. "Back to the Gypsies? To me, it appears you have left them."

"That matters little to you," Bran said. "My life is my own."

"On both points I must disagree," she said. "Your path matters much to me. And your life is not your own. Or have you no faith in our Heavenly Father?"

"Must you speak in riddles?"

"No longer," she said. She pointed again. "Now they approach."

Indeed, there were four men. They were beyond the far edge of the field, cantering toward Bran on black horses.

"Chose between me and them," she said. "You might have your doubts about me, but they are merely doubts. Of them, on the other hand, you can be certain that they mean you harm."

There was no choice for Bran.

"What help do you offer?"

"Give them what they seek," she said. "Once they have it, they will have no need to pursue you."

"I have already told you that—"

Bran stopped, cut short by the motions of her hand as she tossed him a flat, round piece of medal. He snapped it from the air and glanced at it.

The medallion.

"It is a close copy, is it not?"

Bran studied it. The same size, and with similar markings. But not identical.

"A close copy," he agreed.

"My advice to you," she said, "is to give it up reluctantly. That will convince them that it is the medallion they seek."

"After that?"

"Once they depart, go to the stream. You will see a tall oak, once struck with lightning, and now white from years of weather. Wait for me there."

"What if they kill me?" Bran asked. His sore arm was a reminder of how close they had come to succeeding the night before.

"Look," she said. "They wear masks."

Bran looked. Far away as they were, he could see the their faces were covered with dark cloth.

"The masks show they wish to remain unknown to you. Would they go to such effort if they intended to kill you? No. They only seek the medallion. To them, you are merely a pawn."

"And to you?" he asked.

The four horsemen had reached the stone fence, perhaps a half mile distant.

"That is a fair question. Yes, to us, you are also a pawn. For it will be a great service if you send them casting upon a false scent. Yet, you are more than a pawn. You will have the opportunity to test yourself and join us if your heart is right."

"Us?" he asked.

The drumming of horse hooves reached him faintly. His attention, though, remained on her.

"Those who sent your father into this far land."

Again. His father!

"Who?" Bran demanded with great heat. "Who are you?"

She turned the horse with a flick of the reins. She looked back at him and uttered one word before riding away from him and the approaching horsemen.

"Merlins."

1 O

The woman of mystery had predicted correctly. The horsemen let Bran live. They took the false medallion without answering one of his questions. Then they departed, without striking a blow or uttering a threat.

Alone as the morning sun grew hot, Bran completed his task at the fire. Beneath the ashes, protected by a thick layer of packed dirt, was a leather pouch of coins.

These Bran had saved over the years. While Antonio always searched Bran's clothing upon his return from picking the pockets of townspeople, Bran usually hid one coin beneath his tongue. Because there was so little privacy among the Gypsies, Bran found different hiding spots for his growing collection of silver. Since his was the menial task of preparing the firepit, he often chose to hide the coins deep in the protecting soil beneath the fire, knowing no Gypsy would stumble upon his cache there.

With the coin pouch safely in his hand, Bran felt much better. To be sure, he had no home. It surprised him to discover a sense of loss. The Gypsies taunted him, sometimes beat him, and always treated him as worse than a slave. But he had known no other life. Part of him wanted to set off in pursuit of the clan. Better to be lonely among them, than alone in unknown dangers.

What kept Bran back, however, was the knowledge that one among the Gypsies had betrayed him to the hooded stranger. No matter that the stranger's intentions were good. Bran had been betrayed by the clan.

Should he take his coins and wander, letting fortune take him where it may? Perhaps a farmer might give Bran work. Or he could apprentice in a trade. One day, then, Bran might have a secure home. If fortune really blessed him, he might even marry and have a family.

The thought made him smile. It was one of his favorite daydreams.

But he was equally drawn to the woman of mystery. Not her looks, he scolded himself, but the promise of what she knew about his father.

Should he risk travel with her?

Although Bran pondered the question as if there were a decision to be made, he knew deep down that there was only one answer.

Yes. He would travel with her. There were too many questions. If he turned his back on them now, regret would haunt him his entire life, regardless of what fortune brought him.

Questions.

How could she have known that Bran had deceived the four men by tossing a coin onto the cobblestone? Only from the hooded stranger or from the four men. But if from the four men, why had she helped Bran deceive them again? No, she knew from the hooded stranger. Thus, they were friends, if not partners.

The hooded stranger knew of Bran's father. As did the woman of mystery. That alone drew Bran to them.

As did the secret behind the medallion. Why could it matter so much that men were willing to risk their lives? Why could it matter so much that men were willing to kill?

Finally, who were the Merlins? Why had they sent Bran's father into this land?

Bran was determined to learn the answers.

Even at the risk of his own life.

He would go carefully, however, trusting no one and always alert.

That was his decision.

Bran walked to the stream. He washed himself, glad for the cool water.

He searched for the tall, white oak and found it downstream, only a hundred paces walk. Bran settled himself into the shade of the tree.

Despite his best intentions, he fell asleep.

He dreamed a dark dream, that one of the horsemen had begun to smother him. In his dream, he died, falling into a deep, black hole that oddly left him in a state of peace. In his dream, his arms could not move, nor his legs, and flies tormented him by crawling upon his face, flies he could not wave away. In his dream, his tongue grew thick with thirst until the gentle singing voice of a beautiful woman pulled him out of the deep, black hole.

Bran woke, blinking, to a damp cloth smoothed over his cheeks and forehead.

It took him a moment to realize the gentle song was not part of the dream, but belonged to the woman who cradled his head and soothed his face.

1 1

She smiled.

"You are awake," she said. "I feared you might never return."

Bran pushed himself to a sitting position. He croaked with surprise to see the long shadows of evening upon him.

"The sun! Nearly gone! Surely I have not slept all day!"

"I doubt it was sleep," she said. "More likely, a sleeping potion of some sort."

Bran tried standing. His legs failed him and he sat again.

"My head hurts. My tongue is a block of wood."

"Sleeping potion, then," she said. "For I have been with you a good part of the afternoon, shading your face from the sun."

"Potion?" He thought of the sensation of arms and legs like blocks of wood, of flies crawling across his face. "But why?"

"To that," she said, "I have no answer. But I fear the worst."

"The worst?"

"Your medallion," she said. "Someone searched you for it."

"How could that be?" Every answer she gave him only led to more questions. "Those horsemen believe they have it."

"Did you lose the medallion?" she asked, ignoring his question. "Was it taken from you while you slept?"

Bran patted himself, searching. He found the pouch of coins and relaxed. If indeed he had been searched for the medallion, the searcher was not a common thief.

"I told you earlier that I did not have the medallion," he scowled. "How could I have lost it then?"

"As you say," she said.

"Without the medallion, am I of less value to you?"

"Every living soul has value to our Father in heaven," she said.

Again, she spoke of heaven. The Gypsies had taught Bran that it was fortune who smiled or frowned at whim, not a God in heaven.

"Aside from my value to this Father of yours," Bran said, "without the medallion, am I still of use to you?"

She dropped the damp cloth and stood, helping Bran to his feet. He saw her white horse grazing nearby, reins tied to a branch.

"Come to the stream," she said. "Drink."

The sun's light had become golden. It was the quiet part of evening, when the wind died and the green of the trees and fields grew soft and shadowed.

Somehow, being with her made Bran more observant of all beauty around him.

He commanded himself to stop such thoughts. There was nothing he would trust about this woman. It could have been she who drugged him and searched him. After all, she was the one who had directed him to that oak; she knew where to find him. For that matter, he didn't even know her name.

"What should I call you?" he said.

"Rachel," she said. "Rachel of Magnus."

"You know I am Bran?"

She nodded.

Bran crouched at the stream, filled his hands with water, and gulped again and again. After taking his fill, he asked again. "Rachel of Magnus, without the medallion, am I still of use to you?"

He already knew the answer. Of course he was of use to her. Why else would she have stayed with him the afternoon? Especially if it had been she who had searched him for the medallion and discovered it gone. He was simply asking to judge her reply.

She answered his question with a question. "If I supplied you with a good reason, would you be able to trace the medallion's markings on paper with charcoal?"

Bran thought of the days he had stared at the medallion, and the nights he had held it in the darkness, running his fingers over its raised symbols. It was all that held him to his dead parents. The markings were seared into his mind.

"I am able," he said.

"And will you travel with me to Rome?"

Rome. The greatest city in all mankind. Despite his hurting head and great thirst, excitement surged through Bran.

"Yes," he answered. "If you fulfill your promise to tell me about my father as we travel."

"Then," she told him, "you have great value. Greater than you can imagine."

12

Rachel let Bran sit behind her on the white horse. He thrilled at the prospect, for he had never been on a horse before. Only the wealthy afforded such luxurious travel.

Yet a few miles later, Bran decided the wealthy could keep horses for themselves. He sat squarely upon the spine of the beast, and it was not comfortable at all.

"Do we ride to Rome tonight?" he asked. "If so, perhaps I will walk beside this horse."

"Hardly. There is a monastery just over the next hill. We are guests there."

"We?"

"My brother and I," Rachel said. "Edwin. You met him yesterday. First in town. Then at the bridge."

Bran felt secret relief. He had not dared ask about the hooded stranger, fearing she might tell him the man was her husband, or her betrothed.

"He is not hurt badly." Bran said it not as a question, but as an observation.

"He suffered a cracked head and must rest for a week or two. But the monks who nurse him assure me his injury does not threaten his life."

She paused. "How did you know?"

"You showed no signs of worry or grief."

"Gypsy," she said, "it bodes well that you watch things closely and use logic as a tool. I shall welcome your help."

Bran cautioned himself against enjoying the warmth of her praise.

"Again," he said, "let me ask you to begin the tale about my father."

Rachel laughed. "And again, let me tell you that one more night matters little. At the monastery, you shall be fed well. You will be invited to bathe, and after a full night's rest, you and I will begin our journey."

"Just the two of us?"

"Just the two of us," she answered.

"No soldiers to guard us?"

"You are a Gypsy, accustomed to living by your wits. What do you fear?"

Bran nearly gave the answer closest to the tip of his tongue. What he feared was what he did not know about her.

"It is not usual for a young woman to travel unattended," he replied instead. "Bandits along the road will see us as easy prey."

"They will not see a young woman," she said.

"I do not understand."

"Because we must leave Edwin behind to rest and heal," Rachel said, "you and I will travel as beggars. Do you fancy the guise of an old man, or an old woman?"

"What!"

She laughed again. It was a sound that, against his will, Bran was growing to like. "An old man, then," she said. "We shall keep one of your arms beneath your shirt. It will appear as though you are maimed. Better to be seen as totally helpless.

"As for me, I shall pretend to be your wife, still faithful after years of poverty. Does that suit you?"

"Answers suit me," he growled. "And thus far you have strung me along, as a donkey follows the carrot on the end of a stick."

More light laughter from Rachel. "You said it, Gypsy, not I!"

13

An old woman woke Bran from his sleeping mat in a room of the monastery. Bran fell back in surprise as the crone's face loomed over him, such was her ugliness beneath a filthy cape pulled over her head. Her nose was long and twisted, her skin gray and scarred.

What repelled him most, however, was her smell.

Without thinking, Bran put his hand over his nose.

"I'm not the woman of your dreams?" the crone whispered.

He shook his head, blushing as if the old woman had read his mind. The woman of his dreams rode a white horse, had long, reddish-blonde hair, and looked nothing like this smelly old—

"Rachel!" Bran said, remembering their conversation the night before. "Is that you?"

The old woman cackled briefly, then dropped her voice to normal tones.

"None other," Rachel said.

"This is astounding," Bran said.

"Well-placed wax and plant dyes," she said. "We Merlins have a habit of altering our appearance. Lord Thomas told me many such stories. His own father was in disguise. Indeed, that is how he first met his wife, Katherine." Rachel lost herself in daydream thoughts for a moment, as if she were remembering the tales as they were told to her. She shook herself to bring herself back to the present. "But those tales. . ."

Bran grinned, still holding his nose at her stench. "I know now that you are dangling a carrot. I refuse to ask more about the Merlins until we are on the road to Rome."

"You learn quickly," she said. She dropped some clothes on the floor. "Wear these. You will get accustomed to the smell."

"Must the garments be so repulsive?"

"It will keep strangers from prying too closely," she said. "Rome is but a week away. We will not suffer long."

Bran groaned.

Rachel cackled again. "Hurry, my husband. Already the sun has risen. While you dress, I will visit Edwin and wish him well on his recovery. He has promised to follow and meet us in Rome as soon as he is able."

Bran's brow wrinkled. "Rome is a city of thousands and thousands and thousands. How will he find us there?"

"Do not fear," she said. "All you need to do is trust me."

14

During their first hour of travel, Rachel repeatedly corrected Bran for his habit of walking like a young man. As passersby approached, she would urge to him to stoop his back, lean on his crooked walking stick and to put the impression of pain into his steps.

Thus, to any observers, they appeared as poor, aged peasants. Once the road would clear of other travelers, however, both straightened and walked with firm, rapid steps.

"We have the ancient Romans to thank for our ease of travel," Rachel told Bran.

It was a pleasant morning, with a light haze in the sky. Enough of a breeze passed over them to keep them cool, and, more importantly, to take away the stench of their filthy clothing.

"Why is that?" Bran asked, reminding himself not to enjoy her company until the time might come that he could trust her.

"Perhaps you have heard the expression 'All roads lead to Rome?'"

He nodded, although he had not. Life among the Gypsies did

not provide much in the way of learning.

"Well," Rachel said, "all roads do lead to Rome. It was a great empire, controlling lands thousands of miles away. To rule, however, the Romans needed to be able to move armies in quickly at the first sign of revolt. They built cobblestone roads that stretched to all points of the empire. An army of thousands could arrive within two or three months. Such quick action not only stopped revolts, but discouraged the provincial rulers from even starting trouble."

There was a long stretch of empty road ahead of them, winding to the top of a low hill.

Rachel let her thoughts wander. "The Romans were intelligent. You see, they did not believe in ruling by force, but by threat of force, which takes much less effort. The Romans also showed intelligence in another matter. Unlike other empires, they did not strive for total domination of a conquered country. Instead, each country was allowed its own rulers, own customs, and own religions, as long as it continued to pay taxes and tribute to Rome."

Much as Bran wanted to push her to talk about the Merlins, he found himself soaking in the knowledge like a thirsty plant. He considered what she had just told him.

"I think I understand," Bran said after a few minutes. "If you chose force as the way to control, then you must send in an army to occupy the lands. If it takes one army to control one country, and you only have ten armies, then you can only subdue ten countries. But if you rule the way the Romans did — without sending in your armies to occupy that land — then you can add far more than ten countries to your empire. And your ten armies are free to rove where needed."

He grinned in triumph. "On roads which let them move quickly."

Rachel applauded. "You are an excellent student. I can see our time to Rome will pass quickly."

They passed a few more minutes in silence. No travelers appeared over the crest of the hill. They continued to walk quickly.

"Think on this," Rachel said. "Our Father in Heaven placed His Son on earth during the one time in all of history that the world itself was best poised to allow men to spread His Gospel. Had Jesus Christ been born even 50 years before, it would have been too early, for the Romans had yet to subdue Judea. Yet by the time He had been crucified, His followers could take His message out of Judea on Roman roads, into the largest empire the world had ever known. And best of all, this was the first great empire that gave its people the freedom to chose their own religions. This was the one time, then, that the Gospel could have a chance to take root. And of all those local religions, the one true Faith endured and grew through the centuries which followed. How ironic, that this great empire which crucified the Son of God, would soon worship Him."

She stopped, for Bran's face showed puzzlement, even beneath the heavy disguise of old age.

"Yes?" she asked.

"Heavenly Father? Son? Son of God?"

Rachel grew quiet for a few moments before speaking again. "Please forgive me," she said. "I forget you grew up among Gypsies. Who there would have told you about the Christ?"

She shook her head, continuing to admonish herself. "We who have the faith sometimes assume everyone knows the story, and that those don't believe persist out of stubbornness. Instead, I suppose, we need to take the other's view and wonder what needs to be spoken. For the message must be heard and understood before it can be believed."

"Message?" Bran laughed. "You have really lost me now."

"I suppose I have," she said. "But Rome is a week away, and I will tell you all about—"

"The Merlins. And how it is you have such knowledge of times past. I have been a dutiful donkey thus far, letting you dangle the carrot in front of my nose to bring me along this road. I will go no farther unless you begin to tell me as promised."

"The second is simple to answer," she said. "My knowledge of the past? Older Merlins instruct younger Merlins. We call it school. And younger Merlins learn to read at any early age. Books can take us to faraway lands and times and—"

"You can read!" Bran could not conceal the awe in his voice.

"All Merlins are able," she said simply. "It is the best method to pass knowledge from one generation to the next. And once one can read, books themselves become teachers."

Bran stopped her by grabbing her shoulder. "I want to know about my father. I want to know about Merlins. I want to know how I can read. You said perhaps I could become a Merlin. I want that. I want —"

"Yes, I will tell you," she said. "All of it. And soon. But first, we need to find our way past those men ahead. I fear their intentions are not the most kindly."

Bran turned his attention from her to the road. He saw the outline of five men who had crested the hill, a quarter-mile ahead.

As they grew closer, it was obvious by their clubs and swords that they were highway bandits, confident that the isolation of this stretch of road made any travelers easy prey.

15

"What do we do?" Bran asked. His first impulse was to flee. He was not big, but fast. Yet if he outran Rachel, she would be alone against these bandits.

As a Gypsy, Bran knew well the dangers of open countryside. These men could beat, rob, and kill her. They could toss her body into a grove of trees. It might be days or weeks until a passerby happened to notice. And what of it? Who would waste effort searching for the bandits? No one. There was no threat of punishment, no threat of avenging soldiers to stop these men. Without a way for the countryside to be policed, solitary travelers always faced this risk.

If he ran, she faced death. If he stayed, they both faced death. What should he do?

The men walked purposefully toward them. Bran looked back over his shoulder. The road stretched down the long hill. Empty of all others.

"What do we do?" Rachel responded. "We continue to walk toward them."

"But—"

"Fear not," she said. "Merlins have many weapons."

"You have no sword," he said. "And even if you did, there are five against us."

The men were now a couple hundred yards away.

"Sword? Too crude." She placed a hand on his arm. "There is a marvelous substance called black powder, which most of Europe has yet to discover. Charcoal, sulfur, and saltpeter. When sparked, it explodes with fearsome force, sending a flash of white fire that can almost kill a man. I have some of that in my bag beneath this cloak."

"Use it!"

"Or perhaps a sleeping potion," she said, ignoring him. "Much more ladylike, don't you think? I have this hollow reed I can hide in my hand. With a puff of air from my mouth, a small dart flies forth, tipped with the potion. Just a scratch from this dart and a man falls as if struck dead. It appears to be magic and will terrify those still standing. Merlins have used this before."

"The potion, then!" To Bran, the five men seemed as menacing as an entire army. "Use the potion!"

"Or acid," Rachel said, as if she were contemplating what food to serve. "Lord Thomas used that once. He swept his arm and dispensed an acid which blinded soldiers. It is one of my favorite Merlin tales. He —"

"The acid." Bran gritted his teeth. "Use the acid."

Bad enough he needed her help, but to have to beg. . .

She reached into her cloak. "I think not."

"No acid? Then the sleeping potion. Or the black exploding powder. They will be upon us soon."

"No, no, and no," she said. "I prefer the most powerful weapon of all. Wits."

"Excellent," Bran said, slumping his shoulders in resignation.

"We shall slay them with our wits. Most probably they will flee for their lives."

"Actually," Rachel answered, "despite your mocking tone, I believe they will."

16

Rachel pulled a small pouch out of the bag beneath her cloak.

"Turn with me, away from them," she instructed Bran. As he did, she opened the top of the pouch, and poured red powder into her hand.

"Bring your face to my hand," she told Bran.

"What?"

"Step closer."

As he did, she brought her open hand up to his nose, so that the tips of her fingers almost touched his face.

"Do you see anything in this powder?" she asked.

Bran almost crossed his eyes to focus, so close was it to him. The powder was fine, like dust.

"I cannot see anything but —"

With a sudden and unexpected breath, she blew the powder into his eyes.

The blinding pain staggered him. He reached up to rub his stinging eyes. She grabbed his wrists and blocked his efforts.

"Quiet," she commanded. "Too soon they will be upon us. Let

the powder do its work."

"You hideous creature," he snarled, yanking his wrists away. "Have you lost your mind? I am not the one about to attack, but them! Why did you—"

A sneeze took him, a sneeze of such proportion he almost lost his balance. Then another sneeze. Yet one more.

His eyes began to water so badly that tears streamed down his face. A few seconds later, his nose ran too.

More sneezing took him. He could hardly find breath. The next minutes passed as hours. Rachel would not let him wipe away the tears and mucus which flowed from his eyes and nose.

Finally, between sneezes, he saw that the bandits had arrived and stood less than ten paces away. But he could not see them clearly. The flood of tears blurred what he could see of them.

"Help us," croaked Rachel. "Good men, please help us!"

Help, wondered Bran. When men joined together like this, it was not to help those they found alone.

Bran sneezed, widely spraying the contents of his nose.

"We only need a little food," Rachel pleaded in a screeching voice. "Our only way of life is to beg, and the last town sent us away. How can we beg unless we are among people?"

The bandits did not move closer.

"You kind souls are the only ones not to show fear of my husband," Rachel said in her wavering voice. "He does not have the plague. I promise. They were wrong to send us away."

"Plague?" This uncertain question came from one of the bandits. Bran could not decide which, for again a sneezing fit took him.

"Do not be deceived by the red of his face," Rachel said, desperation in her voice. "It is not the fever of Black Death. He is in great health."

"Black Death?" another echoed.

Bran coughed and sneezed.

"Can you spare us anything?" she asked. She wobbled on her cane toward them. "Please, just give me. . ."

Through the blur of his tears, Bran saw them edge away.

"Don't leave," she cried. "Come closer, not farther. Some bread, some coin, that is all I ask."

As one body, all five men turned. They fell over themselves in their scramble to run. Their footsteps clattered on the cobblestones, rapidly growing farther away.

"Did I not tell you?" Rachel asked in merry tones. "They flee for their lives. Already they are almost out of sight."

Moments later, Bran felt hands upon his face as Rachel gently placed a cloth upon his nose and eyes.

"Take this," she said. "Wipe away those tears. Soon the effects of the powder will pass. It is but herbs and roots, ground fine, a special mixture the Merlins have known for centuries."

Bran dropped the cloth. He spun and began walking down the hill.

"Keep it," he said in forceful tones. "Keep your black powder, your potions, your acid. Keep your Merlin tricks and disguises."

"Bran!" She hurried after him.

"What you did was not right," he said, anger obvious in every stride.

"I did not lie," she protested, hard pressed to stay with him. "I told them you were in good health. I am not to blame that they assumed you carried the plague."

"What was not right was how you treated me," he said. "From the moment I met your brother until now, you have both treated me like a child, teasing me with the promise of secrets, herding me like you would a sheep. Now this! Using me with your little trick of powder. Had you asked, I would have agreed, for our lives were in danger. But to blow it in my eyes without warning is. . . is. . . is. . ."

Bran could not remember the last time that anger had taken him to the point of rage. The Gypsies had beaten him, taunted him, humiliated him, yet he always bore it with stoic patience. With them, however, he always understood they were clearly against him. Rachel, on the other hand, had pretended something different, then deceived him.

She placed her hand on his arm.

He shook it off. "I will never hit a woman," he said. "That is the only reason I am not striking you."

"Bran of Magnus," she said. "Will you forgive me?"

What had she just uttered? Bran. . . of. . . Magnus? Did he actually have a home?

"Please," she said. "We must not fight. As two who share the Merlin birthright, we must join together in battle against evil."

Bran stopped. *Merlin birthright?*

"Tell me everything," he said. "Now. Upon this hillside. I move no farther unless I hear it all."

1 7

They moved to sit in the shade of a tree. Bran's face itched from the waxy disguise, but he remained still. So much did he wish to know what she might say, it seemed to his ears that each of his heartbeats were separate peals of thunder.

"Let me begin," she said, "by telling you we have more in common than our Merlin birthright. When I hear the children sing the Dance of Death, I fight to hold back tears. For my mother, too, was taken by Black Death. This was just a few years ago, when the plague swept through England again."

Both of them gave respectful silence to her words. It was the single greatest fear in any person's mind. For good reason, the bandits had fled from Bran and his red face and hard sneezes.

Black Death.

It was a plague which struck so quickly that a person might wake sneezing in the morning, and be dead by nightfall.

Black Death.

It spread like fire touched to straw. All it took was one child in a family to begin the dreaded coughing, sneezing, and high fever.

And half, sometimes more, in that family would be dead within a week.

Black Death.

Towns of five hundred would be reduced to three hundred mourners, with the bodies of the two hundred dead stacked in the streets to be burned as soon as the survivors found strength.

Black Death.

It took its name from those who died, their faces purple and dark in agony.

Black Death.

With Rachel's Merlin education, she could have told Bran that Black Death had taken half the population of Europe in two separate epidemics. Bran's parents taken during the first one in 1348. Rachel's mother taken in the next, 1361. Not only their loved ones. But others. Dead in the millions upon millions. A disease that struck commoner and royalty alike.

Black Death.

Red, rosy faces pocked with rings of pus. Pockets and sleeves stuffed with flowers, for it was futilely hoped that the scent would ward off the disease. The ashes of bodies burned. And the near certainty of falling down dead once the disease struck. Children now danced and sang a mockery of the death's darkness, a dance of death that always brought Rachel to tears as she remembered her dying mother. "Ring around the rosie, pockets full of posies; ashes, ashes, we all fall down."

The breeze of the hillside passed over them. In the sunshine which had burned through the earlier haze, the horror of sweeping death seemed unreal. Yet not even the pleasantness of a morning alone in the countryside could banish the fear of that horror.

It took several minutes before Bran spoke.

"By your own words and by your accent," he said, "it is plain you come from a faraway land. You know, however, my mother fell to the plague. You know about my medallion. You even knew that I plucked coin from the pockets of townspeople. How can all of this be?"

"A letter."

Bran waited. A butterfly dipped and swooped between them. Rachel finally took her eyes from it and answered his unspoken question.

"It was a letter from your father. It took years to reach us, passed and sold from traveler to traveler."

"Sold?"

"The bearer of this letter was promised a half-year's wages for safe delivery to Magnus. Whoever first had the letter decided not to risk the danger of passing through many lands, but instead sold it for a little gold to another who might take it closer. That person in turn sold it again. And so on. Each time, the letter moved closer to our land. Once though, its owner died to road bandits. And the bandit who took the dead man's possessions could not read and had no idea of the value of the letter. He discarded it. A little boy found it, and brought it to his priest, the only man in the village who could read. The priest set it aside and forgot it. Not until the priest died several years later did anyone see it again, finding it among his books. And so the letter's journey resumed, until finally, many years after your father's death, did his words reach Magnus."

"And?" Bran said

She did not reply immediately.

Bran's patience could not be stretched farther. "Why had he been sent into this land?" he demanded. "What of my mother? How did they meet? How did they fall in love? How did he die? What sent her back to the Gypsies without him?"

Although Rachel's face was distorted with disguise, when she smiled sadly Bran saw nothing but beauty.

"It is a story worthy of any ballad," Rachel said. "My dream is to find a love such as theirs."

Again, she forced Bran to wait. This time, however, he saw that she was collecting her thoughts, and he did not interrupt.

"I, of course, have read the letter," she said. "Before leaving Magnus, it was my task to set the letter to memory, for it was considered too dangerous to travel with it, and Edwin and I needed to be able to refer to it. Instead of answering your questions, then, with your permission I shall recite, as surely as if I am reading from it."

"Please," Bran said softly. *It would be as if his father were speaking directly to him from beyond the grave.*

"This is the letter, then." Rachel closed her eyes and began to speak.

18

My father, we have been betrayed. By whom, I cannot say, although as I am near death, I wish I had this knowledge to pass on. The betrayer is one of us. Not only has my life been betrayed, but also the mission upon which you sent me forth from Magnus.

I can imagine you as you read this. A light frown will cross your face, and you will run your fingers through your thick, white hair. Thinking of you thus brings a smile to my face. No matter how grave the crisis, you show no agitation. Bring your concerns to the Lord God you always say, keep in mind the perspective of Eternal Life, and troubles in this fleeting world will never overwhelm.

My father, it is advice I have leaned upon heavily in the last year. Yes, nearly twelve months have passed since I was first betrayed.

It happened thus. Upon crossing the mountains and reaching the plains of northern Italy, I was sent from our small party of travelers into a town to seek provisions. Just outside of that town, I was waylaid and taken into the trees near a river. My attackers wore masks. They began to beat me senseless. I pretended early unconsciousness, hoping the beating would end. When it did, they began to search me. I heard one of them speak of the precious medallion, which I had not taken with me, but left behind safely hidden.

As you reach this portion of the letter, the same question will occur to you as it did to me. How is it that thieves could know of the medallion? Or that they knew it was my responsibility to safeguard it?

Father, you know better than I do that those who expect us in Rome would never betray the cause or the existence of the medallion. Even if one among them were so inclined, none there have knowledge of how we travel, when we are to arrive, or even our appearance. It is impossible for them to know we have entered Italy. The source of betrayal, I concluded, was not among them, but could only be one of those traveling with us.

Yet even as I concluded this, the knowledge appeared of little use because imminent death was upon me. The thieves bound my arms and legs and tossed me into the river. The current took and battered me. Downstream, around a bend, the river pushed me up against a boulder, and there, for a few moments, I was able to draw air.

I would have died, except a woman was washing clothes on the bank. She waded out, and although the rushing water pushed higher than her waist, she persisted. She had a knife, which I found remarkable until later when I discovered she was part of a Gypsy camp. With that knife, she cut my bounds and helped me reach shore.

I was too weak and injured to move. This woman hid me and returned at night to tend to my wounds and to feed me. She kept my existence a secret from the other Gypsies, for they are united against all outsiders. This continued for one week, while the Gypsies camped outside of the nearby town.

Her name is Maria. Father, I confess this was no ordinary woman. I have heard you talk about your first encounters with the woman masked in bandages, the woman who, later unmasked, became your wife and my mother. It seemed to me that the love growing between us was of the same greatness. I knew that if you were near to advise me, you would have blessed my intentions. I asked this woman to wed me, and she agreed.

We found a church and a priest married us before God. In so doing, however, we both became fugitives. Me, from the betrayer among us. She, from her clan who was furious that she had joined with an outsider. The stakes were even higher and their fury even greater than I had dreamed, for she had kept hidden from me her position among them. They considered her a princess, and were determined to bring her back, determined to kill me.

As fugitives, however, we had a mission. The medallion was still hidden among those traveling to Rome. I did not feel safe openly returning to them, for this would let the betrayer know that I was still alive.

It took a month to find them. Then, at night, I went into the camp and took my horse away from them. The medallion I had hidden in a hollowed out portion of my saddle. Maria and I fled.

Even with the medallion in my possession, however, I did not consider it safe to proceed to Rome. Although I still did not know who it was, the betrayer would be waiting for me, and could easily claim instead I was the betrayer. To all appearances, it was I who had disappeared, then returned in the night to steal the medallion.

Furthermore, a handful of Gypsies were still in relentless pursuit.

Maria and I could not rest easy, and spent months moving day by day to avoid capture, until without warning, the hand of Black Death struck me. Now, as I near death, I see no other course except to take the risk of writing this letter and praying it does not fall into the wrong hands.

Father, I doubt I will live to the end of this week. It fills me with sadness, knowing I will never see the deep green valleys of Magnus, that I will never hear the sweet voice of my mother singing, that I will not jest with you again. If fills me with greater sadness to leave Maria. Our love is a more wonderful joy than I imagined any love could be. The joy and mystery of it surely reflects the love that God our Father has given us all.

As I face death, I thank you for your teachings, for passing along the great hope of Christ, dead then risen. Without that hope, this life would have no meaning. With it, I can joyously look forward to an eternal home in the warmth of Love greater than all love. With the hope of Christ, I know that death is merely a painful heartbeat, leading me into God's presence. With this hope through Christ, I know that when Maria leaves this world, I will be there waiting for her. Father, you were right. Death has lost, and now serves to show us the power of our risen Lord.

Thus, I face death without fear. Maria will return to the Gypsy camp, taking with her this letter, the medallion, and our child, whom she carries in her womb. We have decided that there among the Gypsies she will best be able to give birth.

I take satisfaction in knowing the one who betrayed the secret of the medallion has no knowledge of Maria being in my life. Because of this, it is not possible that anyone knows the location of the medallion. It shall remain thus until this letter reaches you.

It is Maria's greatest wish, and mine, that somehow, she will find a way to return to Magnus once the child is born. If the Lord grants us this, Maria will return to you the medallion. I know without asking that you will treat her as your daughter.

As a safeguard, should she be unable to rejoin you in Magnus, I have made provisions to ensure this letter will reach you without her. At the seal of this letter, I shall pledge a half year's wages to the person who brings this letter to you unopened. You can know then, if this letter reaches you without Maria, you will find the medallion among the Gypsies.

Yours in the Lord who sustains us. . . your son, Christopher.

19

When she finished reciting the letter, the sudden silence was a loud as a clap of hands, and it brought Bran back to the reality of the hillside where he sat beneath a tree.

Many thoughts went through Bran's mind, but he only spoke one. "It is not me you sought, but the medallion."

She understood his question and the slight bitterness in his tone.

"You are wrong," she said. "Yes, the medallion is of great value. But your grandfather wishes very much to have you rejoin him in Magnus."

"Me? A Gypsy mongrel he has never seen?"

She smiled. "You will be welcomed as royalty. For in Magnus, you are."

Bran's puzzlement was obvious.

"Your father wrote this letter to his own father," she said. "Your grandfather. Does that not mean anything to you?"

Bran's mind had been full of the bitter sweetness of hearing his father's last words.

"I suppose," Bran said slowly, "because he loved his father."

"You can have no doubt of that," Rachel said. "But think. This is no ordinary letter. The bearer of it earns a half year's wages. Much of its message pertained to the mission and the medallion. Would such a letter go to a peasant farmer?"

"Perhaps not," Bran answered.

"It would go to the lord of the kingdom," Rachel said. "Thomas of Magnus. Your grandfather. Who cherished you from the moment he knew of you. Do you not think then, that part of our task was not only to find the medallion, but to bring you back to Magnus?"

Bran turned his head away from her. It would not do for Rachel to see that he blinked away tears. He composed himself before speaking again.

"If Thomas is my grandfather, I am then a Merlin?"

"No," she said gently. "No person is born a Merlin. To be sure, to be born among the Merlins helps greatly, for children of Merlins are taught from an early age. Yet to become a Merlin a decision must be made by each child when ready."

"I see," he said. Although he did not. "You will explain more to me?"

"As we travel," she said.

Bran would ask for more than explanation of the Merlins. The letter clearly showed a trust his father and grandfather had in God. Why? How? Bran wanted to know more. And he wanted to know more about this Christ. How could a man die and then rise again from the dead? Much as he wanted to discuss these matters, Bran was compelled to ask her a different question. The obvious question.

"Who betrayed my father? Do you now know?"

"That is as much a mystery to us now as it was to your father."

"Could it be the same who betrayed Edwin? Who drugged and searched me at the tree?"

"I think it likely," she said. "Which is why we travel in disguise."

"The medallion," he said after some reflections. "Tell me about it."

Rachel paused a moment before answering. Etched over her silence was the tittering of birds and the rustle of tall grass in the breeze.

"It is part of a map," she finally said. "Of that I can tell you no more until we reach Rome."

There was such firmness in her voice that he knew further questions would be of no use.

As if to keep him from pressing her, she stood. "Shall we begin?"

He rose and followed her back to the road.

Christopher and Maria, he thought as he walked alongside her. *I now know my parent's names. What a gift. Maria and Christopher.*

Bran's joyful mood lasted the entire day. He realized he had begun to trust Rachel. This, too, gave him joy. Rachel had brought him the knowledge he had wanted his entire life. Best of all, this knowledge was far better than he could have dreamed. His grandfather waited for him with love!

Bran's joy did not diminish as he fell asleep. They had stopped at a roadside inn, and she had produced the coin needed for a meal and one night's lodging.

Alone on his straw bed, Bran smiled into the darkness, thinking over all he had learned. He now understood more about the Merlins. They were like a clan, except without the hatred and suspicion that Gypsies felt toward outsiders. Merlins prized knowledge and wisdom, and strived always to apply it in pursuit of what was good and true.

Sleep began to take Bran. The warmth of his joy was almost as comforting as a blanket.

I was born into family of royalty, he thought for the hundredth time. *I have a home that awaits me.*

Life is a wonderful mystery, he told himself in his final moments before sleep.

Bran's joy did not last long. For when he woke, it was to a sack over his head and rough hands holding him.

20

A hand pressed against Bran's mouth before he could scream. His arms were pinned against his side.

He fought and twisted. He kicked out to feel a satisfying thump. He heard a muffled curse.

A blow rang his ears. He shook off the pinpricks of white pain that lanced his eyes and twisted more. He lashed out with his feet, this time hitting nothing but air.

Another blow to his head. This one harder.

Bran guessed that two, maybe three people were holding him down. What chance did he have, fighting blind?

He stopped fighting.

Beneath the hood, mouth held tight, Bran panted for breath through nostrils flared as much from fear as from his efforts. Was this an execution? Would a dagger slice through his ribs next?

Bran waited for the burning slice of steel. Instead, hands pushed against him.

He tried to make sense of what he could feel. Two pairs of hands held him down. Another pair searched the clothes he wore beneath the single blanket.

No words were spoken. Not from Bran, for the hand on his mouth was unwavering in pressure. Not from his attackers.

The search ended.

The hands, however, did not release him.

Bran strained to hear. It sounded like one of the attackers was now searching the tiny room. The shuffling sounds continued until the searcher had gone through the room twice.

Bran heard a grunt. A grunt of disappointment?

"Nothing," came a harsh whisper. "It is not here."

"The straw then," came a whispered answer.

The hands pushed him onto the floor and held him there with great strength. Bran could imagine his attackers leaning down on him with the full force of all their weight.

He heard the third person rip apart the mattress. Then he heard the jingle of coin. They had found his small pouch of silver and gold.

The coins were scattered on the floor.

"Not among these," the harsh whisper announced. "Where can it be?"

"Enough," the answering voice whispered. "We have risked too much time in here."

The hands released him, just as quickly as the attack had taken him from sleep. Quiet footsteps left the room.

Bran gasped for a mouthful of air, sucking the fabric of the hood against his face. He pulled it away and yanked the hood off his head.

Were it not for the hood and the light of a single candle left in a holder that illuminated the scattered coins, Bran might have been tempted to believe he had awakened from a vivid nightmare.

He knew, of course, what the attackers sought. The medallion.

21

Much time passed until Bran found the strength to move. He rubbed his face, sick with the only conclusions he could draw.

They had traveled all day in the hot, heavy disguise of old, poor peasants. Who else could know they were here, then, but Rachel? Who else could have sent them into the room but her?

His betrayer was Rachel.

It was now obvious to Bran that she hadn't believed him when he said he did not have the medallion.

He thought more. He decided she would not have been able to send these attackers into his room the night before, at the monastery among the monks. This night, then, had been her first and best opportunity.

Bran gathered his scattered coins from the floor. His hands moved slowly, as if someone else were scooping them into the leather pouch. His mind still fought questions.

Bran began to wonder if everything she had told him during the day was as false as her motives.

He did not wonder for long. Immediately he told himself it was ridiculous to believe that he could be the grandson of a lord of a kingdom in a faraway land.

Rachel could easily have lied, too, about his parents. As a Gypsy accustomed to fleecing peasants, Bran knew the best lies were the ones that people desperately wanted to believe. Bran could think of no lie he would want to believe more than a wonderful tale about a mother and father who risked their lives for a great love.

A new thought struck. Earlier, against the road bandits, Rachel had spoken of sleeping potion which she herself carried. Sleeping potion. The same sleeping potion that had been used on him only days before?

Bran pondered all of this, growing more bitter and angry at Rachel as the night passed. How much more cruel her lie, to give him hope of paradise then snatch it away.

Then it occurred to Bran that his attackers had not killed him as he feared. He began to wonder about that too.

This medallion must be of such great importance that they could not risk killing him until they knew for certain where the medallion was. Or until he had sketched the symbols for them to read.

A map, Rachel had said.

A map to what?

All Bran needed do was close his eyes to bring back all the symbols on both sides of the medallion. He knew, though, it might be a letter of death to actually put these symbols into charcoal lines on paper. Once they had the medallion or its symbols, his life had no value. It seemed, then, his greatest value was in the knowledge only he had.

If that were true, he decided, he must keep the knowledge to himself as long as possible.

Anger and bitterness gave him resolve.

Whatever this game was, he was determined to win. If the medallion were the only weapon he had, he would use it. He would play along with Rachel, pretending he trusted her. When he finally discovered what treasure the map would bring, then he would find a way to betray her in turn. And take the treasure.

With a grim smile, Bran piled the straw back into the shape of a mattress. If he wanted to win this game, he needed rest.

He blew out the candle and slid beneath his blanket.

He closed his eyes.

In the morning, he would gaze upon the innocent smile that she used to hide her treachery. He would smile back with equal innocence. And with equal treachery.

22

From the north, they came into Rome along the Via Flaminia—the Flaminia Road—with Rachel drawing pictures with words, so that Bran could almost see the marching lines of Roman soldiers as they returned triumphantly from the wars of earlier centuries. He could nearly hear their measured footsteps along the stones and imagine the throngs of citizens and slaves cheering them on as they entered the city.

Before they reached the Tiber River, both sides of the road had been rolling hills of pasture and olive groves with occasional stone farm houses. Once near the Seven Hills, however, buildings began to press upon them, as did a stream of travelers on foot, mule, horse, and cart.

Bran and Rachel allowed themselves to be swept along with the confusion and bustle of travelers. For Bran, it was almost overwhelming. Much as he had heard about the great city, he never dreamed there could be so many people, so many great buildings.

He had long given up asking Rachel their destination in Rome, so he remained silent, drinking in the sights and sounds and smells of a city of dust and stone in the midday heat.

On and on they pressed, until Bran began to believe the city stretched forever. Through the markets. Into slums of buildings pushing in crooked lines against each other.

Then the road opened. Bran gaped as they passed the Palace of the Popes, yet Rachel did not allow him to stop.

She brought him past great ruins—columns of stone standing alone amidst rubble—then to a Coliseum of such proportions that he believed her stories of men called gladiators who fought beasts or each other in the open arena before spectator-crowds of thousands. He marveled with horror at other stories of believers following the one called Christ, cast before lions and bears to be killed for the amusement of those same spectators. Although Rachel had spent much of their travel talking about Christ to Bran, he still could not understand why men and women and children would choose such a death before giving up their beliefs in the Christ.

During this discussion, Bran began to notice they were now traveling against the stream of horses and mules and carts and stragglers, instead of with it. Soon after, the buildings began to thin, and the green of countryside became open once more.

Bran could not stop himself from asking. "Have we passed through Rome? What is our destination?"

She surprised him by answering without evasion.

"We are now on the Via Appian, the road that a man named Paul took into Rome as he brought the belief of Christ to the Romans."

Rachel pointed to the city wall behind them. "The outer limit of the ancient city," she explained. "Ahead, we walk up this road as it gently climbs the ridge. In three miles, we reach our destination."

"How can you be so sure?" If, finally, Rachel was prepared to speak about that which she had earlier kept hidden, he wanted to press her.

"Before I left Magnus," she said, "your grandfather taught me all that I should memorize as we moved through the city. He taught me how to find the place."

"And how did he know?"

"Many, many years earlier, he traveled the same road."

"Why?" he asked, a thrill passing through him to think he now walked the same path.

"Can you not wait the half hour until we arrive?"

"Arrive where?" he asked, unable to count how many times earlier he had asked the same question.

"Now that we are so close," she said, "I see no harm in answering. Ahead, our guide waits at ancient burial grounds."

23

They stopped in a grove of olive trees, just off the road.

"I am not tired," Bran said. "We need not rest on my account."

Rachel smiled. "My friend, we have arrived."

"Here?" Bran swept his arms to take in the trees, the small shrubs, the tall grass. "How can this be an ancient burial ground? Where is our guide?"

"Patience," she answered. "There, past the trees. That building is our destination."

It was midafternoon now, just past the greatest heat of the day. Despite his irritation and curiosity, Bran was glad to be off the hot, dusty road and in the shadows of the trees as they walked.

As they arrived at the small stone building, Bran snorted. How could this be a destination worth a week of travel in disguise as an old man? It was almost in ruins. Half of the clay tiles of the roof were gone, the other half crumbling. Where a door had once stood, there remained only traces of rotted timber.

"Inside," she said. "There we wait."

"I do not understand."

"You will tonight," she said. "When our guide arrives. He will see the lit candles I place on the window sill and know that after all these years, the Merlins have returned."

Rachel began to pull the wax disguise away from her face. She invited Bran to do the same. She removed her old outer clothes. As did he, grateful to shed the weight and filth. It felt as if he had become a new person.

He looked at Rachel with a sideways glance. He fought a mixture of admiration and distrust. In the dappled shade from branches and leaves of a tree above the ruined building, the softness of her beauty was a wonderful and unwanted distraction.

She moved to a deeply shaded wall deepest in the shade, and sat, leaning back against it.

Instead of resting, Bran paced.

"The small lights of candles this deep among the trees will be impossible to notice so far back from the road," he said. "Only if someone has been watching will they even know we have entered here."

"I am certain we have been watched," she replied. She reached into the cloth sack she had been carrying for their provisions. She offered him water from a leather pouch and bread and cheese.

Bran, however, could not relax. Rachel's serenity and certainty only agitated him more. "For a week, you tell me nothing. Then you promise an ancient burial ground and bring me instead to a ruined building. And now you want me to believe that someone has been watching and waiting. You want me to believe that day by day, year by year, this forgotten grove of olive trees outside of Rome has always been watched."

"Of course," she said. "A treasure as great as the one which waits below us is always guarded."

24

Bells from the center of Rome penetrated the darkness. Bran counted. Ten times. The black velvet of a clear night had long since arrived, and the scattered white dust of stars showed through the gaps in the roof.

Rachel sat beneath the open window. Seven candles were lined across the sill. The flames burned straight in the breezeless air. The candles themselves were nearly stubs. They had been new when Rachel and Bran had first begun waiting.

"Without more candles in your sack, you are sure to be disappointed," Bran said, standing and stretching. "Or perhaps your guide is blind. If indeed he exists."

"Not blind," a voice said from behind him. "Merely silent and cautious."

Bran stumbled backward and spun around. Still, he saw no one.

"Know that here lies united an army of Saints." The voice came from beyond the open doorway, drifting in quietly.

"These venerable tombs enclose their bodies," Rachel recited, equally quietly, and with no fear, "while the Kingdom of Heaven has already welcomed their souls."

Bran watched the opening carefully, waiting for a deeper blackness to show him a person had moved into the doorway. Only the voice entered.

"Here lie the companions of Sixtus who bear the trophies won from the enemy," came the voice. "Here lie the brotherhood of popes who guard the altar of Christ."

Rachel took a breath. "Here too, I, Damasus, confess I would like to be buried were it not for the fear of disturbing the ashes of these holy persons."

Bran waited for the voice to return. It did not. Instead, seconds later, the flames of the candles were extinguished by someone outside the ruined building. Bran jumped and stumbled in the opposite direction.

"Come," the voice said as Bran was recovering himself. "Step outside."

"Fear not," Rachel said to Bran, standing. "He is our friend. And he knows we are his friends. I have replied as he expected. And he as I required. From an inscription on a tomb below."

In the darkness, Bran felt her take his hand. He allowed her to take him outside. She dropped his hand.

The outline of the man in front of them was tall, the shoulders bowed.

Without a word, he began to walk away from them, his footsteps soft in the deep grass.

Rachel followed. Then did Bran.

Fifty steps away, he turned, directly into a hedge.

"Protect your face with your arms," he said. "No need to scratch your face."

Again Rachel followed with Bran behind, groping as a blind man in the deeper darkness of the branches. His hands found Rachel's shoulders. She reached up and squeezed his fingers.

Her shoulders dropped. Then Bran understood. They were

walking down steps. Slowly. It did not take them long to reach the bottom. Only a slight creaking warned Bran that a door had been opened. The faint glow of a torch showed narrow tunnel walls.

The tall figure stepped inside. Rachel did not hesitate to do the same.

Bran paused. What madness was this? Entering the depths of the earth with the woman who had betrayed him twice already?

Rachel stepped back and found his hand again.

"You will not be met with harm," she said. "Give me your trust."

Trust was last of any possession he would grant her. Only his vow to return treachery with treachery gave him the courage to move ahead.

Once he was inside, the guide closed the door behind him.

All three walked toward the glow of the torch. As the light grew, Bran was able to see more of his surroundings. The tunnel was hardly higher than the guide's head. The tunnel walls were narrow; Bran could stretch out his arms and his fingertips brushed both sides.

The tunnel turned once, and the light grew even brighter. They proceeded another dozen steps. In that short space, two other tunnels broke off in different directions.

Bran saw, too, that ledges had been cut into the tunnel walls. These ledges were about the length of a body, only a couple of feet high, and a couple of feet deep. Every few steps, there were three or four ledges on each side, one ledge above the other and above the other. Some ledges were plastered over, contents hidden. Some were empty. Some contained wooden boxes. Other ledges had shrouds, and walking as quickly as he could to stay with the others, Bran could not determine what the thin, ghostly cloth covered.

Bran remained silent and followed, unable to make sense of it.

The tunnel turned once more before they finally reached an open area, lit by the flames of the torch set into the wall.

For the first time, Bran clearly saw the guide. An old priest. In simple black garb.

"Greetings from Thomas of Magnus," Rachel said, stepping forward and formally embracing the man. "And greetings from my brother Edwin who was unable to travel with us. My own name is Rachel. This is Bran."

"Greetings and welcome," the guide said. "My name is Julius. After all these years, welcome to the hidden catacombs of St. Callixtus."

"Catacombs?" asked Bran.

"Yes," the guide said. "Burial chambers for the followers of Christ during the time of the great empire. Here, in twenty miles of tunnels, forgotten over the last four centuries, are the remains of over a half-million dead."

25

Bran shuddered. The ledges dug into the walls made sudden sense to Bran. *Bodies.*

The guide frowned. Bran could see him closer now. The man's face was thin and bearded with gray.

"I was told to expect a young woman," Julius said. He turned to Rachel and spoke hardly above a whisper. "And of course, Edwin, whom I would have recognized. I am sad to hear he was not able to join you. The presence of a third person, however, is a surprise. As is his question. How is it he does not know of the catacombs. Is he not one of us?"

"I wish that he were," Rachel said. "But that is a matter for his grandfather Thomas to decide. As for now, we need him greatly."

Julius nodded gravely. It impressed Bran that Julius did not express doubt. Rachel was far younger than he, and a stranger. Merlins, Bran decided, respect each other greatly, regardless of station in life.

"It was Bran's father," Rachel said, "who first began the journey here. He was the keeper of the medallion. When he disappeared, Thomas believed him lost, all these years. And then the letter arrived in Magnus. . ."

Rachel explained. The air in the tunnels was still and cool. The soft glow of the torchlight showed there was beauty even in the shadows of her face. Bran watched and listened, captivated by her presence and outraged at her calm lies.

He wanted to tell Julius that Rachel was the betrayer, seeking the medallion for herself. But Bran knew patience would pay greater rewards. He listened as she finished the story.

"So you and Edwin spent the better part of a year in the north, searching the gypsy clans for word of a fair-haired gypsy," Julius said. "And you have found him, along with the medallion given him by his father Christopher, may his soul rest in peace."

"Bran does not have the medallion," Rachel said. "He cast it away, so that it would not fall into the hands of those who attacked my brother."

Julius let his shoulders slump. "Surely you know all of this is for nothing without the second medallion. Mile after mile of these tunnels wind beneath the city. There are four levels. Not even I, who have spent my whole life searching these tunnels, know them all. Daily, I must walk with pieces of chalk in my pockets, marking the walls where I have been so that even I will not get lost. How can we find the treasure without the second medallion?"

"He will sketch it for us," Rachel said. "He knows the symbols by heart."

Julius shook his head. "Did Thomas not explain before you left Magnus? It is not sufficient merely to find where the jewels of Callixtus are hidden, but the medallions themselves serve as keys. There are two slots in the wall, one for each medallion. Once both medallions are insert, it springs a lock, and the hidden door opens."

Jewels of Callixtus? Bran felt his heart beat faster.

"I do understand," Rachel said. "Thomas explained it to me very clearly. The ancients devised a cunning system to keep the treasure from thieves. Supports behind the walls will collapse if the door is not opened on its hinges. We cannot dig to get the jewels, for not only will they be lost, but the entire portion of the tunnel will fall upon us."

"This then, is the reason for my despair," Julius said.

"Edwin and I have given our problem much thought," she said, removing from her shoulder the sack she had slung over it by straps. "Before we left him behind, he suggested to me a solution. All it requires is a Merlins' bag of tricks."

Bran knew this was the sack which contained her exploding powder, the blinding acid, and sleeping potion for darts. He would not be surprised at anything she pulled from it. Except for what appeared in her hands.

It was merely a lump of wax.

"Julius," she said. "Here is our second medallion."

He steepled his fingers and regarded her thoughtfully.

"Once we find the location, we melt this wax and pour it into the slot. After it cools, we gently pull the wax free. It should hold the shape of the medallion. From it, we make a mold. From the mold, we form another medallion."

"It may suffice," Julius said. "It just may suffice! In the early days, thieves would not have had the time that you and I have. Yes, it may take a several days for us to make a new medallion, but now centuries later the tunnels are ours alone."

Both turned to Bran.

"All we need," Rachel said, "is your sketch. Julius has the other medallion. With it, we can move through this maze to the Jewels of Callixtus."

"Yes," Julius said. He could not hide his excitement. "Perhaps even within the hour. Sketch it on the dirt of this floor, and Rachel and I shall proceed."

"No," Bran said. "You will not proceed without me. Furthermore, explain to me what it is we seek. How it happens to be there. And how my grandfather knew of it."

"Young man," Julius began. "Words mean so little against what is the prize of centuries and against what will greatly assist the Merlins over the next centuries."

Rachel sighed. "Julius, I am afraid he is more stubborn than a team of mules. I know him well enough to recognize that when he speaks in such a tone, he cannot be budged."

"Then I will tell you," Julius said with a sigh louder than Rachel's, "about the catacombs and the jewels of Callixtus."

26

"It began during the first century after Christ's death," Julius said in the modulated tones of one Merlin instructing another. "After Paul reached Rome with his message of hope, a growing number of slaves and citizens began to convert to faith in a risen Lord. Most were buried in common cemeteries, among nonbelievers. By the second century, rich families of converts made room on their estates for the burial of poorer Christians. Excavations begin then, for the rocky ground of these estates—vineyards and olive groves—consist of soil over top of tufa. It. . ."

Julius had been watching Bran closely, for he saw his student's puzzled expression.

"Tufa," Julias said, "is volcanic rock. Soft and easy to dig. It hardens once exposed to air. If you look closely at these walls, you can see the marks of the workers' picks."

He allowed Bran the chance to examine the walls by torchlight before continuing.

"The workers removed this rock and dirt by basket. You have already seen the ledges they carved to make room for bodies."

Bran nodded.

"There are many catacombs in Rome," Julius said. "This, the catacomb of St. Callixtus, is among the largest. From the third century on, the Church of Rome administered these tombs, and for many years a deacon named Callixtus was the custodian."

Julius walked several steps. Bran merely watched.

"Come with me," Julius said, growing more enthusiastic in the role of teacher. He took the torch from the wall. "Your eyes will teach you better than your ears."

Bran followed first this time, with Rachel behind.

Julius led them farther down the tunnel until they reached another opening, much larger than where they had first stopped. He swept the torch to let Bran see the full extent of the widened walls.

"The Crypt of the Popes," Julius whispered. "We do not worship them as saints; however, they were men of God and deserve much respect. Antherus, Fabian, Lucius, Eutichian. And Damasus."

Torchlight showed an arched roof of brick and marble columns supporting the roof. There was an altar, and a table in front of a large sheet of smooth marble covered with inscription.

"Go ahead," Julius invited Bran. "Step forth. Read the inscription. It is the one you heard Rachel and I recite to each other. Translated from the Latin, of course."

Bran squirmed. He did not want to admit he had no knowledge of Latin, let alone that he could not read.

"He has already heard it," Rachel said with a light laugh. "Let us not waste his time by straining his eyes in this poor light."

"My apologies," Julius said with a slight bow.

For a moment, Bran was tempted to throw aside all his bitterness toward Rachel. She had been gracious, preserving him from embarrassment.

"The Christians worshipped here," Rachel said quickly to keep the silence from becoming awkward. "Not only did the catacombs serve as a burial place, but also as a church, for there were times the Roman emperors persecuted the Christians."

"Yes, Rachel," Julius said, "whoever taught you, taught you well. Christians worshiped here and used it as a place of refuge during those difficult times. Imagine how cruel the Romans could be. Covering Christians with tar and hanging them on a post before lighting them so they would be human torches."

Again, Bran found himself wondering about the determination of people who would rather cling to beliefs than save their lives.

"Why kill them?" Bran asked. "Rachel told me that the Romans encouraged different beliefs and customs."

"Ah, yes," Julius said, with the enthusiasm of one who enjoyed debate but has not had the chance for some time. "But once it began to take root, there were some Emperors who found these new beliefs threatening."

"They are only beliefs," Bran protested.

"Beliefs much different than the religions tolerated by the Roman emperors," Julius countered. "The other religions compromised and adapted themselves to the whims of officials. The other religions were simply private affairs, serving the inner needs of those who selfishly preferred vague spiritual pronouncements."

Julius stopped and raised his forefinger, as if addressing an assembly. "But Christ's message was much different. It was radical and rejected the cults of the emperors, bringing a total renewal to each believer, and in so doing, threatened to change society."

Julius took a breath. "You see, it was revolutionary to preach that every man, even slave, is brother to the other, and that we are all created by God."

He gasped with mock horror. "Imagine! Preaching that all we have should be shared among the poor. Preaching that every man should love every other man as a reflection of God's love for us. Then actually acting upon it!"

Despite his suspicions, Bran could not help but be entranced by Julius. His manner had changed from stooped old man to one flushed with energy. If this was how Merlins learned, Bran would enjoy the chance to become one of them and. . .

He shut his mind to the thought. No, Bran had already decided on his action against Rachel and those she represented.

"More revolutionary," Julius was saying, "these followers of Christ taught His message that the poor should not be abused, and that justice must be the goal of those in power. How could an emperor with a hardened heart and wealth built upon the backs of thousands of slaves tolerate such a belief?"

Julius resumed walking. As they entered the narrow tunnels again, he pointed from side to side, from ledge to ledge. "All these buried here were welcomed during their lives by other Christians. Rich or poor, ugly or beautiful, they were all loved. In life then, they found freedom. And here. . ."

Julius paused again. ". . .here in death they found freedom to be buried as they wished. The Romans preferred cremation, but the Christians did not. Over the centuries, they all found refuge here, during their lives and after, as a place of rest for the bodies they left behind as they journeyed to heaven."

"Heaven," Bran whispered, more to himself than to be heard.

"Heaven," Rachel whispered, closer behind him than he had expected. "Where God the Father waits with love as surely as your grandfather waits for you in Magnus. With open arms. And love that does not depend on what you have done, but on the simple fact that you are. And Bran, heaven is much, much lovelier than Magnus. You will be treated as royalty in both places."

Inside, he shook off her words. She was a snake of treachery. Outwardly, however, he nodded with a smile.

Julius was had gained a few steps on them in the narrow tunnel.

"This is a delight," Julius said over his shoulder. "I have been the sole custodian of these catacombs for so long, it is wonderful to be able to speak of them."

"They are secret?" Bran asked, following.

"Only because they have been forgotten," Julius answered. "The empire fell, and by the eighth century, the popes were unable to provide protection for the relics in the catacombs. Gradually, the relics were moved to churches in the city, for the Christian faith had triumphed to become the accepted faith. The catacombs were no longer needed now that churches could openly serve. Within decades, landslides and vegetation covered most of the entrances to these catacombs. Two hundred years later, no traces of them existed to the world above."

"Except to Merlins?" Bran asked. They had nearly reached the first opening where Julius had gathered them before the torch.

"Yes," Julius said, "Except to Merlins."

He glanced nervously at Rachel. "How much does he know?"

"Some," she said, "but not all. Let me explain the rest, for he had asked about Thomas and the jewels."

Julius nodded assent.

"Bran," Rachel said, "when you become one of us, you will learn our complete history, which begins before the time of a great king named Arthur. For now, you will have to accept what I tell you. Merlins are dedicated to using knowledge to strive for good. Merlins are dedicated to preserving knowledge and passing it from one generation to the next. Because of evils in this world, we keep this knowledge in our own way and in many different places. Julius here is one of us, far, far away from Magnus, but no less dedicated. Here in Rome, Merlins like Julius have guarded knowledge for centuries. These catacombs have served them well to hide not only their presence, but their books."

"And the jewels of Callixtus," Bran said.

"And the jewels of Callixtus," she agreed. "He was an honorable man. Much in gold and jewels was donated to the cause of the faith from not only those rich believers buried here, but all Christians. Can you imagine how much wealth might be here from a half-million believers? Legend says it is enough to buy a kingdom. Maybe two. Callixtus hid these riches during the times of persecution—"

"Here in the catacombs," Bran interrupted.

"Yes," Rachel said, not at all irritated. "Callixtus devised the map of the two medallions. He also brought in craftsman to build the hidden crypt and the invisible door that needed those two medallions as a key, knowing that the miles of tunnel would make it impossible for them to ever find it again."

Bran nodded. Already, he had lost all sense of direction, and they had barely penetrated any of the maze.

"Knowledge of the jewels of the crypt of Callixtus has always been passed from generation to generation among the Merlins, but it was almost considered a fanciful legend, even here in Rome where the Merlins have always had one of the medallions safely guarded. Then Thomas, your grandfather, found the other medallion in the hidden tunnels beneath Magnus, with a decayed parchment directing the finder to the catacombs here in Rome."

"And he sent my father, his son, with that medallion."

"Yes," Rachel said. "He was too old to travel to Rome himself, although in his lifetime he had been here to visit other Merlins. You already know the remainder of it. Now do you understand why your medallion had such great value?"

"But I don't understand who else would have known of it to betray my father." Although Bran was sure that Rachel was the treacherous one of this generation, it did not explain who it had been all those years earlier, when his father had traveled to Italy, to die in the arms of the woman he loved.

"Druids," Rachel whispered. "They have always existed. Darkness to our light. Among us, they still exist. Hidden, even to those of us who are Merlins."

Bran tried to absorb what he had learned.

Julius shook Bran's shoulder, gently. He handed Bran a dagger.

"Now, my son," Julius said. "If we have satisfied your curiosity, will you sketch in the earth here what you remember of both sides of the medallion?"

He reached into his pocket and pulled forth a medallion, similar in size to the one Bran's parents had left him.

"Adding the symbols on my medallion will give us a map," Julius said, "I know the tunnels well enough that if your rendering is accurate, I have confidence we will find the hidden crypt."

Bran did not reply, but knelt, placing his knees squarely on the ground. With the tip of the dagger, he began to scratch patterns in the packed dirt.

A half hour later, they stood in front of the crypt of the jewels of St. Callixtus, deep within the earth.

27

Hours later, Bran woke in the room that Julius had provided him in a small house near a church beyond the olive grove. He and the priest shared one room. Rachel had another.

After finding the crypt on the second level, it had taken less than half an hour for Julius and Rachel to make a mold by pouring melted wax into the opening for the missing medallion. Once the wax had dried, and they had taken the impression of the medallion, the return trip to the surface had been a short twenty minutes of triumph and hope in the eerie quiet of the catacomb tunnels.

During that time, Bran had watched Julius carefully, making observations and marking them in his mind. When they reached the small house, Bran drank three cups of water before lying down to sleep.

It was no accident, then, that Bran wakened during the stillest, darkest part of the night. He'd known the urgency of a full bladder would rouse him from sleep at the hour he needed.

Upon waking, Bran remained on his straw mattress. He did not move until he was satisfied Julius was in deep sleep. The priest snored with such enthusiasm, Bran immediately decided there was little fear the old man would wake.

Bran crept out from beneath his blanket. During all the time Bran had watched Julius, the priest had been careless only for a moment, while Bran had pretended sleep. Because of that, Bran knew where to search.

He squatted beside the wall at the foot of the priest's bed, alert for any movement from the old man. With slow steady movements of his hands, Bran felt along the wall and pried loose a stone which covered a hiding hole. Bran removed what he needed and set the stone back into place.

Still silent, Bran stepped from the room.

He had no intention of leaving the house, however. He groped along the walls to find the entrance to Rachel's room.

He listened carefully to the rhythm of her breathing. It did not alter as he entered her room. She had placed her sack on the floor beneath the window. Bran lifted the sack, stepped back out of her room, and finally outside of the house itself.

A half moon gave little light, but with it, Bran was able to find what he sought in the depths of her sack.

Bran set aside what he needed. On his toes, and alert for any sounds, he returned to the inside of the tiny house. As carefully as he had taken the sack, he returned it to where Rachel had left it on the floor.

Rachel's breathing had not changed. Briefly, Bran thought of Rachel's happiness at finding the crypt of the jewels of St. Callixtus. Remembering the peace and beauty in her smile softened his heart. He wondered if he should continue with his course of action. As his determination wavered, Bran forced himself to also remember the sack over his head at the inn, and the hands which had roughly searched him. Only by reminding himself of her treachery did he keep his resolve.

He stepped outside of her room again.

He stopped to listen again to her breathing. No matter how skilled an actress she might be, there would be some change in the rhythm—slight or not—if she woke. Bran knew this, for many were the nights he had stolen away from the gypsies to be alone beneath the stars.

He heard only the continued softness of her deep breaths.

He stepped outside again, pressing himself against the front of the house to keep the pale light of the half moon from casting any shadow.

When he reached a tree almost against the house, he moved beneath it. From there, he crept farther away from the house.

Once he believed himself safe from detection, he walked through grass wet with dew to the next tree.

After a few minutes, he made a direct line toward the olive grove.

Bran felt no fear moving through the deep shadows. Night, after all, was an old friend. And there was plenty of night left. With satisfaction, he judged that far more night remained than what he needed before made an equally stealthy return to the house and the two who peacefully slept inside, unaware of his departure.

28

Julius spent the entire next day in Rome, returning just before sunset. He found Bran and Rachel sitting beneath an olive tree, where they were almost finished with a simple meal of cold chicken, soft bread, and the juice of pressed apples.

"The silversmith did just as you suggested, Rachel," Julius said. "First, he molded a clay ball around the wax impression, leaving a small hole. When the clay had dried sufficiently—which was an insufferable wait—he slowly heated the ball in an oven, until all the wax ran out the small hole. Then he poured molten silver through that hole into the clay mold. When the silver cooled, he cracked the mold open. And look!"

Julius opened his hand to show gleaming silver. The medallion. An exact copy of the one which Bran had been given so many years earlier by his father.

He leaned over and handed it to Rachel. "Carry it for us."

She clenched it in her fist, then stood and briefly hugged the priest. Stepping back, she said, "Surely it will fit the opening, just as the wax did. Yet unlike wax, the pressure of hard silver will be enough to open the lock."

Julius nodded. "I see no reason to delay. What ceremony have we to fulfill? None. The jewels have been sitting in the dust of centuries. This very hour we shall begin to polish them."

"And portion them also?" Bran asked, still sitting.

Julius smiled indulgently. "I know you can hardly believe our intentions for all this wealth. But as we told you last night, half will remain here. And half will reach Magnus. Yes, the love of money is the root of all evil. But money itself can do much good. Wise Merlins will find ways to let this money work for the good of God."

Rachel tugged at his hand. "Come, rise. I am as anxious as Julius to open the crypt."

Bran stood and dusted his lap of bread crumbs. "You are certain you want me to join you? After all, you now have what you sought from me."

Through treachery, he nearly added.

"Bran," she said, "I can think of nothing I want more than you by my side."

She blushed as the meaning of her words struck them both. "That is. . ." she stuttered. ". . .as we return to the catacombs and open the crypt."

Julius chuckled. "Young man, it seems to me that you have a beautiful woman who regards you as more than a friend."

"Hush," she said to Julius. But she did not hide her smile for Bran.

Bran only felt confusion. Rachel had the medallion now. What more could she gain by acting in this manner?

Unless, he decided, she meant further treachery in the depths of the catacombs. After all, with the bodies of a half million lost in the dark tunnels, what difference would one or two more make? If she wanted the wealth, with Bran dead, and perhaps Julius too, the jewels would be hers. And the secret of her treachery would never leave the catacombs.

Bran smiled and hid his thoughts. Then he spoke truth.

"Rachel," he said, "I, too, can think of nothing better than standing at your side as we open the crypt."

29

They retraced their steps from the night before. Through the olive grove to a thick hedge, down hidden steps cut into rock, to a small door. Inside, a slow-burning torch waited for them.

Bran followed Julius and Rachel. He was determined to remain behind her. A dagger in the back was not how he wanted to die.

The torch showed small white "X's" on the tunnel walls. Julius had marked the path to the jewels the night before.

Bran would have preferred to walk with his eyes closed. For occasionally, one of the ledges would be open to sight, the result of plaster falling away over time. Where there was no coffin, there would be heaped bones, ghostly soft in the light of the torch, with strands of hair shining near the skull. Century after century the remains of these bodies had lain undisturbed, long since cleared of any decay.

Bran did not like these reminders of mortality. Much as Rachel had spoken to him of heaven, much as she had explained to him that Christ was the Son of God and had lived among men to give them a home in heaven, Bran was not inclined to share her faith and hope in life beyond death. Her witness of Christ, after all, had little significance when she used a pretense of devout goodness to hide the core of treachery.

No, Bran preferred Gypsies to her hypocrisy. Theft was a way of life for them, one into which he'd been raised. At least with them, there was consistency. If one of them had attempted to steal the medallion from Bran, he would have only had himself to blame. After all, around wolves, a man took steps to protect his sheep. But when a man began to believe the wolf was instead a friendly dog, only hollow bitterness resulted when the sheep were attacked.

Bran remained deep within his brooding thoughts as the three walked in silence, with only the scuffling of their footsteps echoing through the tunnels. It gave him a dark satisfaction to think that he might return to Rachel the treachery she had given him.

They followed the white chalk marks, easily visible, through turn after turn after turn. Fifteen minutes later, they arrived at another wide opening.

It was no more than five steps wide and five steps deep. Two other tunnels lead away from the opening, so that it appeared to be hardly more than a junction. There was a flat wall, free of ledges, between those two tunnels, barely wider than a man's shoulders.

This section was different from any other section of wall in the entire twenty miles of twisting, confusing maze. Waist high, the sign of the cross had been scratched into the soft lava rock. This cross was hardly bigger than the length of a thumb, and impossible to see unless a person knew exactly where to look.

Directly above the cross, just below the roof of the tunnel, were two tiny slots, so close together that both could be touched with one hand of a person standing below and reaching upward. Again, unless a person knew exactly where to look, with the torch light directly upon the slots, they were invisible. Indeed, the night before, it had taken Julius ten minutes of searching to find them.

"I am almost afraid," Julius said when they stopped. "For all my brave talk about needing to fulfill no ceremony, it seems that after so many centuries, perhaps something of importance should happen before we test the hidden lock."

"Not a ceremony," Rachel suggested quietly. "But prayer. I can think of no better place or time."

Julius nodded.

Along with the other two, Bran bowed his head and joined hands.

As Rachel opened her heart in whispered words, Bran let his mind wander. He felt no guilt over this. The God she spoke to was not his God.

He thought of the afternoon she had wiped his face with a damp cloth, pretending concern that someone had induced him into a potioned sleep beneath the tree. Had she expected her beauty to blind him? That he would not realize she had directed him to the tree and no other person would have known he would be there?

He thought of the morning after his head had been put into a sack and after he had been searched for the medallion. Across their break of fast, she had smiled innocence and asked him if he had slept well. As if he didn't know she had sent the ruffians into his room.

He thought of all the times during their days of travel that she had spoken to him of tales of the man called Jesus, telling Bran of miracles and of love and compassion and of a man risen from the dead.

He thought of how he had smiled and nodded during those hours, enjoying the tales as entertainment, but refusing for a moment to believe her further in anything she said.

All this ran through Bran's mind as she prayed.

Along with one more thing. He had darts in his pocket, along with the tiny tube which gave him the power to propel those darts. For during their hours of travel together, he had made certain to ask her to explain the Merlin tricks in her sack.

Now, if she tried to betray him once more by attempting to kill him here in the catacombs, he was prepared.

Rachel finished her prayer.

All three raised their heads.

And found themselves not alone.

"Edwin!" Rachel gasped.

Her brother stood nearby, watching them with a cruel smile beneath his red beard. He wore a cloak over fine clothes. In his right hand, he held a huge broadsword.

He bowed. "No less than I."

"But you. . .the monastery. . .how. . ." She could not find words.

"My dear sister," he said. "I was not hurt at all. It simply served me well for it to appear as such to the world."

In a flash, Bran understood how stupid he had been. He began to withdraw his hand from his pocket. If somehow he could bring his hand to his mouth, and fire one of the darts already in the tube. . .

"Tut, tut," Edwin said to him. Edwin raised the broadsword and pressed the point of it against Rachel's neck. "I would prefer you all remained as motionless as stone."

"But Edwin!" she said.

"Don't prove to be tiresome," he told her. "Haven't you realized it by now? I am here to claim for the Druids what centuries ago St. Callixtus left behind."

30

"Druids?" Her voice trembled.

He laughed lightly. "Druids. Far wiser than Merlins. From boyhood, my efforts have been for their cause. For they do not insist on sharing wealth with those in need, but keep it for themselves. And I, for one, have no difficulty looking out for myself before others."

"You are the betrayer," she said. "The one that Bran's father described in his letter."

"Edwin was here on the earlier journey," Julius confirmed. "Years later, it is he who attempts it again."

"Who else?" Edwin rolled his eyeballs in mock dramatics. "Is it the so-called Merlin logic which let you both draw that conclusion? Or the fact that I have a sword at your throat?"

He snorted. "Why else did I arrange to have it appear that I had been attacked on the bridge when I first met with this Gypsy? I could not merely rob him of the medallion myself. No, I needed to cast suspicion elsewhere."

Bran gritted his teeth. The tube and the dart with sleeping

potion was no more than a quick movement away from his mouth. Yet if Edwin's sword pressed any harder against Rachel's throat, it would draw blood.

Bran dared not risk any movement. When he had first met Edwin, heavy clothes concealed much of the man's bulk. Here, dressed in lighter fabric, it was obvious that Edwin was a bull of a man, with muscles like large ropes on his forearm. One twitch of those powerful wrists and Rachel was dead.

"Just like years before when I sought the medallion from Christopher," Edwin said. "I hired strangers to be thieves. With no knowledge of why I wanted the medallion, or of its worth, a piece of gold each was all it took. Only on this occasion, I hired them to rob me and the Gypsy together."

He spat. "The mongrel outwitted them. I needed to promise them more gold to help me further."

"It was your idea that I go to Bran," Rachel said, hardly above a whisper. "Your idea that Bran give them a similar medallion to fool them. Yet all along you were their master?"

"Brilliant, was it not? It was one more way to ensure you did not suspect me. While the monks were in prayer that day, I stole away from the monastery and found the Gypsy by the tree, according to the instructions I had given you to give him. There, I first searched him while the sleeping potion kept him unaware. When I did not find the medallion, I concluded he had hidden it nearby. Which did not bother me. For I only needed to continue to play the role of an injured man at the monastery. After you both departed from the monastery, I stayed but a half day. It allowed me to follow you, unsuspected."

"It was you," Bran said. "You who sent the men into my room the night in the inn."

"No less."

"The night in the inn?" Rachel asked Edwin.

"I was searched again," Bran said to her. "I thought you were the betrayer. I thought you knew of the search and were hiding it from me. I am truly sorry I did not trust you."

Edwin laughed. "What pathos. This amuses me."

He laughed again. "Yes, Rachel, my young and innocent sister. That night at the inn, the hired strangers helped me thoroughly search the Gypsy and his possessions. It would have been much simpler to have the medallion. I would have easily arrived in Rome long before you and found a way to take the other medallion from Julius. When I knew the Gypsy truly did not have the medallion, I simply went ahead to Rome and waited for you. It had been my own suggestion, after all, that the Gypsy sketch the medallion's symbols. I knew one way or the other that you would lead me to this crypt. After Julius departed the silversmith today, a small bribe gave me what I needed to know. A medallion had been cast. All I had to do was follow."

Julius had begun to edge away. Edwin pressed the sword harder into Rachel's throat, and she sucked in a breath of pain.

"Don't move, old man," Edwin said. "Let us enjoy this brief time on my stage. You can all admire my deceptions."

An alarming thought hit Bran. Edwin would not be in this mood to boast unless he had already decided none of the three of them would ever leave the catacombs.

"Who did you hire among the Gypsies to betray me?" Bran asked. Any time he could steal was precious if Edwin meant to kill them.

"The one named Marcel. I believe he was jealous of you. He was strong, he said, but you were quicker and smarter, and he hoped you would die."

It had never occurred to Bran that anyone would think that highly of him. In a strange way, it made him feel good that someone like Marcel had felt the need to throw harm Bran's way.

"What will you do with the jewels of St. Callixtus?" Julius asked. Perhaps he, too, realized that the longer Edwin spoke, the longer they lived.

"We have a bold plan," Edwin said. "If the wealth of these jewels is as legend says, the Druids will sweep kingdom after kingdom in open revolution."

"Impossible," Rachel said. "Kings and soldiers will defeat you if you move openly against the people."

"Not if Black Death strikes the royal families and the papal courts."

"What!" she said.

"Come, come, Rachel. As a Merlin you certainly know what Thomas and his searchers of knowledge have been able to determine about the plague. Somehow it is passed from person to person. One family members drinks water and passes the cup to another. Both die."

He arched an eyebrow. "The Druids know this too. We have soaked the bodies of the diseased in barrels of water. This water we will distribute in the wells of royal families in all the lands. Kings, queens, princes, princesses, cousins, jesters, all the royal courts will be taken by Black Death. In the power struggles that follow, we will reign supreme. Legend says there is enough wealth among the jewels of Callixtus to buy a kingdom. We shall use it instead to pay soldiers who will allow us to take a dozen kingdoms!"

"And in so doing," Julius said, "you risk beginning another plague across all the lands. Thousands upon thousands will die."

Edwin shrugged. "Less people for the soldiers to overcome."

"Evil has blinded you," Julius said. "But it is not too late to turn back. God forgave Moses, David, and Paul. The three greatest men of the Bible, all murderers who were taken back into the fold of believers. If God can forgive them. . ."

Edwin's face twisted with hate. "Shut your mouth, old man."

"I cannot. Surely your soul is worth more than any wealth."

"Give me your medallion, Julius, before I drain her life's blood."

Slowly, with shaking hands, Julius reached over and placed the medallion in Edwin's free hand.

"You have my thanks," Edwin said.

Without warning, Edwin stepped sideways. He flicked his wrist to turn the blade outward, and with the swiftness of lightning, hit a hammer blow against Julius's skull with the butt of the handle of his sword.

The thud of metal against bone sickened Bran.

Julius fell backward from the force of the blow. Bran's hands shot out to catch Julius as he toppled. Bran staggered backward to hold the man's weight.

"Drop him," Edwin commanded Bran.

Bran eased the old man to the ground. He heard strained breathing from Julius. The blow had not killed him.

"Troublesome mongrel," Edwin growled. "I told you to drop him. I expect you to obey me."

Edwin brought his sword back.

Bran had nothing to help defend himself against the heavy steel edge. When he'd reached for Julius, the tube and dart had fallen from his hand to be lost in the darkness of the tunnels.

Edwin advanced. The sword swooped with a sideways slash.

Bran jumped back, sucking his stomach as deep as he could. The edge of the sword ripped his shirt. But Bran could move back no farther. The tunnel wall pressed upon him.

Edwin brought the sword back again.

31

"No," Rachel said, her voice another weapon of steel.

Edwin glanced back at her.

She held the shiny medallion between her thumb and forefinger. "This is what you want. Not his blood."

"I shall take both," he said. "His blood and the medallion. Where could you cast it from here that I cannot reach?"

She did not answer with words, but tipped her head back and placed it in her mouth. She smiled, and swallowed.

"Now," she said, stepping halfway into the closest tunnel. "It is mine to keep. And while you strike him, I shall flee. All I need is a three-step lead to lose you in this maze."

Edwin dropped his arm in resignation. Bran relaxed. As did Rachel.

It was a mistake.

Edwin kicked Bran in the stomach and used that kick to push off toward Rachel. As Bran fell, clutching himself, Edwin dropped his sword, dove toward Rachel and wrapped his arms around her waist.

Edwin threw her down. Her head hit the ground first, stunning her.

Before Bran or Rachel could react, Edwin spun back and grabbed his sword again. With his foot, he rolled Rachel toward Bran. Julius was still motionless to the side of them.

Edwin stood above Rachel and Bran, pointing his sword in their faces.

"Permit me to gloat," Edwin said. "I think such quickness is uncommon, is it not?"

Still on the ground, Bran put his arm around Rachel to protect her from Edwin.

Edwin laughed at his pitiful effort. "So your heart belongs to her, does it? What a shame I shall have to split her open to retrieve that medallion."

Rachel shrank back into Bran's arms.

"Who wishes to die first?" Edwin asked. "Who wants to watch the other die?"

"You need not kill her to get what you want," Bran said.

"Certainly. I have no patience. I want the second medallion now."

"I have what you need," Bran said. "Take it from me."

Surprise flickered across Edwin's face. "You had it all along? But I searched you. Twice. I shook out your clothes. Your shoes. Everything."

"I'm a Gypsy," Bran said. "Always suspicious. I hid it the same way she did."

With slow, painful movements, Bran struggled to a sitting position. Because of the agony of his stomach, the effort nearly gagged him. Still on the ground, he leaned over, and removed his right shoe. He shook it, and a medallion fell onto the floor. Bran tossed it up to Edwin.

"You have both medallions," Bran said. "Take the jewels. Not our lives."

"I think not. It is much easier to slay you than go to the effort of tying you both while I search the crypt."

Edwin brought his sword up again.

"What if the crypt is empty of jewels?" Bran asked.

The huge broadsword wavered. "Impossible."

"Not if I entered here in the dead of last night and plundered it myself," Bran said. "I had one medallion. Don't you think it would be child's play for a Gypsy to steal the other from Julius and return it while he lay sleeping?"

Edwin's eyes narrowed. "Then why come back today with these two?"

"Satisfaction," Bran said. "I thought Rachel had betrayed me. I wanted to watch the pain in her face as she and Julius walked into an empty crypt. They would never suspect me of the theft. Later, I intended take the jewels at leisure from where I have them hidden."

Edwin drew a deep breath. He thought for several seconds. "No," he said. "You are lying. I kill you both."

Bran smiled. "Then you shall never see those jewels. When I am dead, who will there be to tell you where they are hidden?"

Bran smiled again. "Five large sacks of jewels, Edwin. Another five smaller sacks of silver and gold. It was no easy task to move them elsewhere in the catacombs. Out of the thousands and thousands of tombs, in the miles and miles of tunnel, where might they be?"

"You lie," Edwin said. Yet there was uncertainty in his voice.

"Hold the sword to my throat while Rachel opens the crypt," Bran said. "Then step inside and see for yourself. If I tell the truth, you give us our lives in exchange for the jewels. If I lie, then kill us both."

Silence. Deathly quiet silence.

"Stand," Edwin finally said. "Both of you."

They did, slowly. From his own pocket, Edwin took the

medallion Julius had given him, and flipped it to Rachel. Bran handed her the second medallion.

Then Edwin spun Bran around, gripped his shoulders from behind with one arm, and placed the blade of his sword against Bran's throat with the other.

"Open it," Edwin commanded coldly to Rachel. "One false step and I spill his blood."

32

Rachel stepped forward. She stood on her tiptoes to reach toward the slots high up on the wall. With a medallion in each hand, she pressed them both into the slots at the same time.

There was the slightest of sounds, a light click that was only heard because the tunnel itself was so silent.

Then creaking.

It seemed the entire wall began to move. It slid inward, perfectly balanced on rolling balls. Had the situation not been so grave, it would have been a moment to marvel at the intricate and clever craftsmanship of the men who had labored on it centuries earlier.

The interior was dark.

"Hold the torch high," Bran said. "Give your brother a clear view of the emptiness inside."

Rachel took the torch and stood to the side of the opening. Yellow light flickered into the giant crypt. It was the size of a small room. The roof was arched, the inside filled with coffins.

From outside, still holding the sword to Bran's throat, Edwin spoke. "You said sacks of jewels. Yet I see coffins."

"I pulled the sacks from the coffins," Bran said. "Take me inside with you so that I cannot run away. Together, we will find those coffins empty."

Edwin hesitated.

"I cannot run," Bran said. "Rachel will not flee and leave you to slit my throat. I want you to see them empty. To know I have moved them elsewhere. For Rachel and me, it is our only hope."

Bran paused. "And your only hope of ever getting the jewels of St. Callixtus."

"We go forward," Edwin said. "Slowly. Remember, I carry the sword."

Bran shuffled forward, keeping his feet so close together his legs rubbed as he walked. He stepped through the exact center of the opening.

Edwin kept his grip on Bran's shoulders, and followed.

Bran thought of the Gypsy Marcel, and the balancing act across the rope. It was a matter of perfect timing, of total concentration.

And Bran forced himself to relax, waiting for the single split second that he needed. Any earlier or any later than the one-half heartbeat of opportunity that was about to arrive, and the sword blade against his throat would draw deep.

One step.

Two.

Three.

Then it came.

Edwin grunted a curse of startled pain, and staggered sideways. With the quickness of hands that made him faster than any Gypsy, Bran grabbed Edwin's wrist, pulling the deadly sword away from his throat.

For long, terrible moments, they were frozen like that. Both of Bran's hands braced against Edwin's strong wrist. Edwin straining to draw the sword inward. Bran could not push it any farther away. Edwin could not pull it closer.

Bran gritted his teeth with effort. His two arms against Edwin's one. The man was strong. His hot breath washed over Bran's neck.

"Die, Gypsy," Edwin said. "Die."

How much longer could Bran hold the sword at bay?

Five seconds.

Ten. Fifteen. Twenty.

Finally, slowly, Edwin began to lose strength. The mighty arm dropped away. The wrist loosened its grip on the sword. It clattered to the ground. Edwin toppled to his knees, then collapsed completely.

"Bran!" Rachel cried from behind.

"No!" he shouted without turning. "Don't step inside!"

It was too late. She was already running toward him. Then gasping with pain.

Bran slowly turned, careful not to move his feet away from the exact center.

"My feet," she said, stumbling as she neared him. "They have been pierced!"

She was in his arms. He held her. It had taken fifteen or twenty seconds for Edwin to fall. Soon, she too, would lose consciousness.

"I don't understand," she said, tilting her head away from him to look in his eyes.

"Nails," Bran said. "Last night, I buried them upright just beneath the dirt. With a narrow path in the center to step through. It was a trap, meant for you and Julius."

"Edwin on the ground," she said. "And now I feel weak. The nails. . ."

Her words grew heavy. "The nails. Were they tipped with poison?"

"Lay your head on my shoulders," Bran answered. "I won't let you go."

"Am I going to die?" she asked.

"Yes," he said.

"Oh, Bran, that makes me so sad. I have come to love you."

With one arm holding her, he used his other hand to stroke her hair as her eyes slowly closed, until finally her body sagged against him.

EPILOGUE

Alone, Bran reached the top of a high hill. The hill itself held only tall grass and the low, flat bushes of the north York moors. With no trees to impede his view, he saw the tops of other hills, far away and lost in a gray mist which only added mystery to the sensations he already felt.

He began to cross the ridge, the wind blowing a wild sensation of freedom across his face and hair. His whole body trembled in anticipation.

Magnus, he had been promised, would open up below him when he reached the opposite crest.

Magnus.

It did not take him long to reach edge of the hill. He stepped forward, and for the first time in his life saw it. A place he had never been, but somehow, to see it now, a place his heart knew had always been waiting. No more would he wander through fields at night to pass away sleepless hours in his own solitary dance of darkness. No more would he feel the piercing pain of utter aloneness.

Magnus.

Deep in the valley below was a lake. And in the lake, an island. With a fortress rising high.

Magnus.

Bran wanted to shout with joy. Could it really be? Home? With his father's father, waiting for him with love?

As if an answer from heaven, sun broke through the gray mist.

Bran took a deep breath. It had been a long time since tears rolled down his face. He dropped to his knees.

That's how the woman saw him when she too, reached the top of the hill. On his knees. In prayer. Slowly, silently, with the wind taking away the sound of her footsteps, she approached him. Again the woman marveled that finally he begun to listen to the instinctive yearning of his soul as it reached for God.

She stood behind him for some time, unwilling to break the moment of complete peace.

Not until Bran stood, did she place her hand on his shoulder.

He did not turn with surprise, as if another instinct had told him she was near.

"Rachel," he said. "You were right. There are no words to describe this. I hope you'll forgive me for wanting to first see it alone."

She moved closer, letting him block the wind, wrapping her arms around his waist from behind him. She rested her chin on his shoulder to look down on the valley, thinking back on what had happened in the six months since they had left Rome to travel by horse and boat to get back to England. Julius, nursed back to health. Arrangements to imprison Edwin. Secret plans for the incredible wealth that St. Callixtus had left behind for Merlins to use for good. And—her chin on his shoulder as a reminder—Bran's sudden growth as he moved into full adulthood. He was close to four inches taller than her now.

"Forgiveness?" she echoed. "The only thing for which you'll

never be forgiven is how you deceived me into declaring my love for you."

"I did not lie to you in the catacombs," he said, slipping into their favorite argument. "For surely, unless the Lord returns, there will come a day when you die."

He was facing away from her, but she heard his grin as he continued the familiar ending to this argument, one she brought on as often as she could because she never tired hearing of what he would say next.

"I pray, however, that day will not arrive until you are an old woman," he said. "And not until we have a brood of grandchildren."

He paused as he always did. "After all, I am not to blame if the sleeping potion from your own bag of tricks took you before I could complete what I had begun to say."

"No, my dear betrothed." She lightly kissed the back of his neck. "You are not to blame."

Rachel stepped back and took his hand.

"Stay with me always," she said as she led Bran down the hill. "Thomas, your grandfather waits. And we have arrived where we belong."

Historical note:

Readers may find it of interest that the Catacombs of St. Callixtus indeed exist in Rome as described, were abandoned and forgotten as Julius described, and were not rediscovered until late in the 15th century A.D.